# A HOMECOMING FOR *Kezzie*

*This story is for Dora Cuollo*

THERESA BRESLIN

# A HOMECOMING FOR *Kezzie*

MAMMOTH

*Also by Theresa Breslin*

Death or Glory Boys
Kezzie
Whispers in the Graveyard (*Winner of the Carnegie Medal*)

First published in Great Britain 1995
by Methuen Children's Books Ltd
Published 1996 by Mammoth
an imprint of Reed International Books Ltd
Michelin House, 81 Fulham Road, London SW3 6RB
and Auckland, Melbourne, Singapore and Toronto

Reprinted 1996



ISBN 0 7497 2592 3

A CIP catalogue record for this title
is available from the British Library

Printed in Great Britain
by BPC Paperbacks Ltd

# Contents


| | | |
|---|---|---|
| 1 | Atlantic Crossing | 7 |
| 2 | Dinner Party | 13 |
| 3 | Arrival in Clydebank | 19 |
| 4 | Homecoming | 23 |
| 5 | Settling In | 29 |
| 6 | Casella's Café | 38 |
| 7 | War! | 45 |
| 8 | The Café is Wrecked | 53 |
| 9 | Peg McKinnon | 60 |
| 10 | Love at First Sight | 67 |
| 11 | 1940: Internment | 73 |
| 12 | Kezzie Learns to Drive | 78 |
| 13 | Lucy Runs Away | 84 |
| 14 | Ricardo Returns | 89 |
| 15 | 1941: The Sirens Go Off | 97 |
| 16 | Blitzed! | 103 |
| 17 | Buried Alive | 109 |
| 18 | Evacuation | 115 |
| 19 | The Sirens Sound Again | 123 |
| 20 | Greater Love | 130 |
| 21 | Travelling South | 135 |
| 22 | Close Manor | 142 |
| 23 | School Lessons | 150 |
| 24 | William | 156 |
| 25 | Bad News | 161 |
| 26 | 1942: The Americans Arrive | 168 |
| 27 | US Hospital | 173 |
| 28 | Life or Death | 179 |
| 29 | Recovery | 184 |
| 30 | New Beginning | 188 |

# Contents


1 Atlantic Crossing 7
2 Dinner Party 13
3 Arrival in Clydebank 19
4 Homecoming 23
5 Settling In 29
6 Casella's Café 38
7 War! 45
8 The Café is Wrecked 53
9 Peg McKinnon 60
10 Love at First Sight 67
11 1940: Internment 73
12 Kezzie Learns to Drive 78
13 Lucy Runs Away 84
14 Rosalie Returns 89
15 1941: The Sirens Go Off 95
16 Blitzed! 103
17 Buried Alive 109
18 Evacuation 115
19 The Sirens Sound Again 123
20 Great Love 130
21 Travelling South 135
22 Close Manor 142
23 School Lessons 150
24 William 156
25 Bad News 161
26 1942: The Americans Arrive 168
27 US Hospital 173
28 Life or Death 179
29 Recovery 183
30 New Beginning 188

# 1
# Atlantic Crossing

'Look!' said Lucy. 'There it is again.'

And she pointed up to where the lone Luftwaffe spotter plane droned above the ocean liner. The ragged sound was an irritant in the hot summer sky, a waspish buzz in a pleasant day.

Some of the American ladies at the side of the boat shaded their eyes to watch. One took her hat off and waved, red and blue ribbons trailing from the brim of her white straw boater.

Kezzie, who was sheltering from the brisk Atlantic breeze in the lee of one of the lifeboats, could now see the pilot quite clearly. Goggled and grim-faced, he gave no signal as he made his second wide arc across their bows.

'He's coming back! He's coming back!' Lucy jumped up and down in excitement beside her. Kezzie frowned and took her little sister's hand.

What made her suddenly afraid? The abrupt blocking of the sun between sea and sky as the pilot completed his turn and passed above them? The sudden darkness, and the chilling of the air?

What instinct made her grab the child and yank her arm so hard that Lucy cried out, 'Kezzie, don't!'

Kezzie turned to face the sea, her eyes following the grey outline of the machine as it banked and tilted purposefully, lining itself up with the ship. Its altitude dropped dramatically and then suddenly the shadow of the plane was sweeping back across the Atlantic waves and racing towards them

'Kezzie, let go!' cried Lucy.

But Kezzie was running now Desperately seeking cover on the bleached white deck of the Atlantic liner, with the quoits scattered at random and the deckchairs set in a long line to catch the sun.

An open door . . . It was a hatch to the crew's quarters, nevertheless, a place of safety . . . And she was inside, dragging Lucy with her as the plane came roaring down the length of the boat.

The noise filled the whole ocean The scream of the engines, the sudden chattering of the twin guns on its forward snout, the frantic cries of the passengers on deck, the shouts of the ship's officers Kezzie put her hands quickly over Lucy's ears and gathered her little sister towards her. It lasted for seconds only. Then silence As if a blind had been drawn, a lamp abruptly turned down The happy conversations and jolly waves on the promenade deck, the playful teasing between young men and girls, the laughter of the children, all shuttered in a moment of time.

And it seemed to Kezzie, when she thought about it afterwards, that although it wasn't until the beginning of September, nearly two months later, that the Second World War started officially, it had been on the cruise liner travelling home from Canada to Scotland that the war began for her.

'Scare tactics,' the captain's voice boomed out from the ship's speakers almost immediately 'Be assured, there was no serious threat at any time We were keeping a close watch on him He had his guns aimed high, and had overshot the deck before he fired An irresponsible act to try and alarm us But are we upset? His laughter echoed in the air 'I should think not Now, I want to see all of you at our celebrations tonight Paper hats must be worn No exceptions Everyone to be there, from two to ninety-two A prize for the best hat.'

Notices were quickly posted all over the ship There was to be an informal party after dinner, their last night at sea before they docked tomorrow in Glasgow It was a way of restoring morale after the shock of the incident earlier Although no one had been injured, the atmosphere aboard had changed completely Few passengers had stayed on deck despite the daylight of the long summer evening People crowded in the lounges or chatted in groups on the stairs and companionways.

'This is an American ship,' one man with a southern drawl declared angrily 'How dare they frighten our women and children? They'd better not try to tangle with Uncle Sam We'd lick them faster than it'd take to whistle "Dixie".'

There were murmurs of approval from his audience And in every part of the boat the talk was the same

'Let them come,' Kezzie heard a very elderly Englishwoman proclaim in a tremulous voice We beat them once, we'll do it again

The speaker must be at least eighty years old, Kezzie thought As she led Lucy along to their cabin, she smiled, imagining the old lady dressed like Queen Boudicca and driving a chariot into battle.

'What's happening?' Lucy asked as Kezzie washed and then dressed her in a pretty frock

'We're going to a party,' said Kezzie firmly, as she combed her little sister's blonde curls

Kezzie had told Lucy that the pilot of the plane had made a mistake She certainly was not going to worry the child by mentioning the threat of war in Europe Her sister had recovered well from her traumas and illness of the last year At seven years old her understanding was limited but she was still very sensitive to atmosphere

Kezzie patted her on the head 'Play with your doll, pet, while I get ready'

She picked up Lucy's old rag doll and gave it to her. We've travelled far together, the three of us, Kezzie thought as she smoothed down the doll's skirt and adjusted its hat. She remembered the terrible winter of 1937 just after their father had been killed in a pit accident in Scotland. Herself, Lucy and their grandfather had been turned out of their tied house in the miners' rows. The only shelter they could find had been a bothy on a neighbouring farm. With Christmas approaching, and in dire poverty, Kezzie had been determined to make Lucy a special gift. The nights she had worked late, cutting up precious linen, stuffing those arms and legs and plaiting the woollen hair! It had been worth the effort and sacrifice. The doll, whom Lucy had promptly named Kissy, not only gave her little sister great joy, but, Kezzie believed, had actually saved the child's life.

While Lucy played with her doll Kezzie changed into smarter clothes. She put on a dark blue suit with a full skirt. The jacket was edged in black piping with corded frogging on the front and fitted closely under her bust. Underneath she wore a white high necked blouse. As she pinned up part of her brown curls on the top of her head, she looked in the long mirror which was fastened with brass studs to the door of their cabin. A tall dark-eyed girl gazed back at her. Kezzie hardly recognised herself from the gawky skinny person with tumbled hair who had left Scotland barely ten months before.

The crew had organised music, games and some ice-cream and jelly to try to dispel the anxiety which now pervaded the ship. There were tables set out with cardboard, paper, scissors, raffia and ribbons. Kezzie helped Lucy make herself a red top hat which promptly slid over her nose as soon as she placed it on her head.

Kezzie laughed out loud

They found a quiet place to sit away from the crowd where Lucy could eat her ice-cream Before the music and dancing began the captain made a speech of welcome and then spoke of the earlier harassment

'They'll find that we're not so easily intimidated,' he declared 'If it comes to a scrap then they'll find we're ready Ready and willing '

Rousing cheers came from the floor of the room Kezzie glanced around her Men and women were nodding in agreement Some of the smaller children were waving little flags made from coloured paper Everyone seemed happy and enthusiastic at the thought of war Why then was she uneasy? Her grandfather had fought in the First World War. He rarely spoke about it When he did, it was to lament the terrible loss of life 'Nothing glorious about it at all,' he had said

Kezzie thought again of the plane She recalled Lucy's excitement, she who had never seen an aeroplane before What had the pilot's thoughts been, surveying their upturned faces as he circled above them? Had he misunderstood the intentions of the lady waving her hat? Perhaps taken it as an angry gesture of defiance, the sight of the colours, red, white, and blue enraging him? Why was it, that a recent invention like an aeroplane was immediately adapted and used by man for the purpose of war and killing? Kezzie's one vivid memory of today was the American lady's hat floating away on the grey Atlantic waves, the bright ribbons bedraggled and sad

Kezzie shook her head and firmly pushed all these thoughts away She and Lucy were going home to Granddad Returning, after an absence of almost a year, to stay with him in his tenement house in Clydebank She would be cheerful and try not to think about war The music had begun Already children and adults were taking the floor The tunes were mainly popular and light a combination of British traditional and modern American

Kezzie felt a touch on her shoulder She looked up A tall young man with very black hair was standing just behind her chair

'May I dance with you?' he asked

# 2
# Dinner Party

Kezzie glanced at the dance floor, crowded with couples laughing and talking together, and dancing. Then she looked up at the boy who had spoken to her. He wore an elegant dinner suit with a white shirt and bow tie, and had the dark good looks of an Italian. He gave Kezzie the impression that he would dance very well.

Reluctantly she shook her head, and indicated Lucy who was eating her way through her bowlful of ice-cream. 'I don't wish to leave my sister on her own,' she said.

The young man smiled down at her. The effect of his smile, bright white teeth in his tanned face, was startling.

'Of course,' he said politely. 'May I sit with you for a little while then?' he asked.

Kezzie hesitated. She was almost sixteen years old, it was 1939, and she had spent some time in North America where the social customs were much more relaxed. However, she wasn't sure if it would be the done thing in Europe. Most people on the ship were travelling in family groups or with male escorts She should really say no, but it would be so pleasant to have someone of roughly her own age to chat to, and . . . he was very handsome. She glanced around her uncertainly.

The young man smiled again 'One moment, please,' he said. 'I will return

Kezzie watched him as he crossed to another table where an older man and woman were sitting. He spoke to them and then all three stood up and came towards Kezzie

'I would like to present my family to you' The boy gave

a slight bow. 'My mother, Signora Biagi, my father, Signor Biagi, and myself, Ricardo Biagi.'

Kezzie introduced herself and Lucy, and shook hands with Ricardo and his parents. She invited them to sit down.

'Now we are chaperoned,' Ricardo smiled at her in triumph. 'So everything is swell, no?'

Kezzie laughed at the Americanism in his otherwise perfect English.

'Everything is swell,' she agreed.

Signora Biagi spoke to her. 'You must excuse us,' she said. 'Our English is not very correct, but Ricardo,' she gazed at her son with pride, 'is fluent in both Italian and English. He is a college student,' she added, and stretched across to pat her son's hand.

'Mama,' protested Ricardo, 'You are boasting again' He turned to Kezzie. 'Do you find that your parents do this all the time?'

Kezzie looked at him. 'I wish they could,' she said softly.

As she grasped the meaning of Kezzie's words Ricardo's mother covered her mouth with her hand. '*Zita!*' she exclaimed. 'You have lost your mama and papa, no? Ricardo. Apologise at once. So clumsy,' she scolded him, 'so clumsy and unthinking.'

'I am so sorry, so very sorry,' said Ricardo He looked so comically sad and forlorn that Kezzie almost laughed

'Please don't upset yourselves,' she said quickly 'Lucy and I have some very happy memories and we talk about them often. Our grandfather has looked after us since our father died. He lives in Clydebank, and we're going back now to live with him again.'

'He works in the shipyards?' asked Signor Biagi

'Do you know him?' Kezzie asked in amazement

Signora Biagi laughed. 'My sister tells me, in

Clydebank, *everyone* works in the shipyards.'

Kezzie found Ricardo's parents very easy to talk to. They told her they were going to spend a few months in Scotland to help Signora Biagi's recently widowed sister who owned a delicatessen shop.

'Ricardo will help her manage for a little while before he returns to America when his college starts in autumn,' said Signora Biagi. 'Then I may stay on a bit longer. It depends how she is.' She spread her hands out and shrugged. 'Her son is in the army and stationed in England, so she is very lonely.'

After a few minutes Ricardo stood up. He looked at Kezzie. 'Now that etiquette has been honoured,' he said formally, 'perhaps I will be able to have a dance?'

'I can dance,' said Lucy quickly. She placed her spoon on the table and wiped her mouth with her hand.

'Lucy!' exclaimed Kezzie.

Ricardo laughed.

'It *is* a party, isn't it?' said Lucy. 'And I want to dance.'

'Such a pretty little girl,' Signora Biagi leaned over and stroked Lucy's hair, 'should certainly have someone to dance with her.' She offered her hand to Lucy. 'Dance with me, *piccola*,' she said.

Lucy took Signora Biagi's two hands in her own and they both skipped off across the room.

Kezzie stood up slowly as Ricardo drew her chair out. A sudden feeling of shyness came over her as he led her out on to the dance floor. The band was playing a slow number, and he put his arm firmly around her waist and began to steer her around the floor. Although she was quite tall, her head scarcely reached his shoulder. She had guessed correctly, Ricardo was an expert dancer, and they were soon twirling about among the rest of the crowd. Kezzie relaxed and began to enjoy the feeling. It was fun to glide along with the music. She couldn't remember the last time she had danced with a boy.

And then suddenly she did. And the recollection struck her with such force that she stumbled slightly.

'You all right?' Ricardo bent his head to look at her anxiously.

'Yes,' she whispered.

But it wasn't his face that was in front of Kezzie now. Nor his brown Italian eyes that she saw. She was with the potato pickers at the close of harvest nearly two years ago, on Stonevale farm in the west of Scotland. The noise in the barn, the sweet smell of the charred potato skins, the taste of the scones and the buttered bannocks. And the music . . . the fiddle, and the thudding beat of the bodhrán . . . and she was being swung around the floor by the young Irishman, Michael Donohoe, and his dark blue eyes were full of mischief as he made up some wild tale, with himself as the bold hero slaying a dozen giants, and rescuing a thousand swooning maidens . . .

Kezzie stood motionless in the middle of the ballroom.

'You are tired,' said Ricardo.

'A little,' said Kezzie.

For no reason at all she felt her eyes fill with tears.

'Then we must stop.'

He took her back to the table. Lucy was sitting on Signora Biagi's knee. She was almost asleep. Kezzie gathered her up quickly.

'Thank you for such kind company,' she said. 'I must say goodnight.' She turned to Ricardo. 'Thank you for dancing with me.'

'My pleasure.' He made a small bow.

Kezzie tucked Lucy firmly up in her bunk and then undressed slowly for bed. As she laid her suit across a chair ready for the morning, she fingered the soft woollen material. Dr McMath and his wife Sarah had bought this costume for her, the day before she and Lucy had left Waterfoot, the little village on the far side of the Canadian Rocky Mountains

'It's far too expensive, Kezzie had protested

'When you wear it, think of us, they had replied

She had thought about them practically every day over the last fortnight They had become as parents to her and Lucy during their year in Canada Taking them into their home, caring for Lucy when she was ill, employing Kezzie in their surgery And more than that, Kezzie thought much more They had given out freely of their love, spontaneously and without hesitation, easing from her own shoulders the terrible strain she had suffered during the weeks she had searched for her sister, when Lucy had been lost in Scotland and ended up in an orphanage in Canada

They would have liked her and Lucy to stay on with them, Kezzie knew that They had in fact offered to help Kezzie to go to university and realise her own dream of being a doctor, but Kezzie had decided to take Lucy back to Scotland Her grandfather was old and had been deeply affected by the death of his son, their father nearly two years ago He needed her and Lucy now

Besides . . she herself had a strong urge to come home, felt that it would be good for Lucy to find her childhood again They might, in time, return to Canada, a country where ambitions could be fulfilled, dreams were born and came to life But at the moment, Scotland, despite the impending trouble with Germany, was the place they had to be

As she lay down that night Kezzie hoped she had made the right decision

Towards midnight Kezzie awoke Lucy was standing beside her bed She had her doll clutched in her hands

'Kissy's frightened,' she said

Kezzie stretched out her arms Do you think a cuddle

would help?' she asked

Lucy nodded Kezzie took the doll and gave it a long hug Without letting go she regarded her little sister gravely, then she pulled back the bedclothes

'You'd better come in and help me watch over her,' she said

They lay together with the doll tucked between them In a few moments Lucy fell asleep again Kezzie lay awake for a long time She felt the heavy seas of the Atlantic give way to quieter waters As the ship edged its way round the Mull of Kintyre it seemed to her that its movement had altered, the heaving dip and roll of the ocean changing to the quiet flow of the Firth of Clyde And as she closed her eyes she sensed the slow deep current which was pulling her and Lucy back to Scotland

# 3
# Arrival in Clydebank

Lucy and Kezzie were the first passengers on deck the next morning as their ship made its stately journey up the Clyde to the dock at Glasgow.

'Will Granddad be there?' asked Lucy, pulling on Kezzie's hand as they stood at the deck rail. 'Will he? Will he?'

'Hush. Hush,' said Kezzie irritably. 'How do I know? Perhaps he will be working at the shipyard. He's very busy.' She looked down at her little sister, and felt her annoyance flow away from her as she saw the upturned anxious face. 'I've got his address in Clydebank. Don't worry, we'll see him soon.'

He'll be there, Kezzie thought, as she saw the summer sky lighten from the east. The docks and wharfs and water reflected the glow of the rising sun and she watched the buildings slip past The long warehouses and offices, shops and factories, and tumble of cottages along the riverbank guarded behind by tall tenements.

He'll be there, she thought.

She knew that he *was* busy. He had told her in his letters to Canada Rearmament work was flooding into the shipyards and factories, revitalising the industrial heartland of Scotland. Firms were receiving government orders as the country prepared itself for a war. People were working again. Even the small knitwear factory in Shawcross, where she herself had been employed for some months, had increased production. Miss Dunlop, the secretary, had written to Kezzie in Canada telling her that they were now making hundreds of socks and gloves for soldiers and sailors. The wind whipped up the estuary and Kezzie shivered. She took her shawl from her own shoulders and wound it around Lucy.

'There,' she said. 'Now put your hands in your cony muff.' She pointed to the little tube of soft white rabbit's fur which Sarah McMath had stitched herself.

Lucy stuck one hand away, but with the other she kept a firm grip of Kezzie's fingers. Kezzie didn't say anything, despite the fact that she knew the child must be cold. She only pulled her close to her and tucked the little girl in against her skirt. Lucy had blossomed in the last few months in Canada. The good food, the loving care of the McMaths, living in that clean wide country had all helped restore her health. But she was still insecure, afraid of the dark, the unknown, anything new. And now she clung to Kezzie, and without fuss Kezzie stroked her head and talked to her quietly,

'Do you see the birds in the water?' she asked her, pointing to where some ducks bobbed and dived by the edge of the river. 'Don't they look funny with their bottoms in the air? Look at that one. He's stolen a piece of food from his brother. Isn't he naughty!'

So Kezzie passed the time calling out the names of everything she could see as the boat moved further towards the heart of the city. On either side they saw houses and bowling greens, grey streets, lanes and wynds, with soft hills beyond, rolling green and golden with a ripening harvest. And above them the aching cries of the seagulls welcomed them home.

There were more people on deck now. The rails were becoming crowded with the other passengers, all of them craning to see some part of this great city.

Kezzie herself could feel excitement rising within her; her thoughts, like the river, becoming more congested the further upstream they moved. The memories of her journey out to Canada How unhappy she had been! How anxious and sick with worry! She hardly recalled looking at the sights at all. Her head was so filled with impatience at any delay, willing the boat to go faster to catch up with the immigration ship which Lucy was on

The crew were getting ready to dock, moving around the foredeck, the officers calling out instructions Kezzie pressed close against the rail, determined to be in the best position to catch the first glimpse of her beloved Granddad There were groups of people on the quayside. Clusters of families, old folk and young children, some businessmen, horse-drawn traps, a few motor cars waiting.

He would be there She knew he would. She scanned the faces. Looking for a tall man, white haired. A sudden recollection of how he had looked one night arguing politics with his cronies clicked in her head, like a snapshot from a photograph album. His cap to one side, his pipe gripped in his fist as he made his point Maybe he wouldn't wear his cap today, just hold it in his hand perhaps? She searched among the waiting friends and relatives Perhaps he was there and she hadn't recognised him Was her memory faulty? It was almost twelve months since she had seen him last He might have changed She certainly had Her face was less peaked, her skin browner, and she was taller and stronger.

He would set himself apart, she suddenly realised, not mingle among the crowd She looked around the dockside He would pick somewhere separate, a place where he would stand out, knowing that she would be searching for him, desperate for a sight of his face She and Lucy both

Her eyes flicked along the length of the quay, past the officials and welcome groups There were the luggage trolleys . . . a loading bay with tackle and hoist . . . the cargo shed . . . and . . . then, a raised platform for a crane-fixing.

A tall broad figure stood there, red kerchief knotted at his neck, bareheaded, arms waving high above his head.

Kezzie gasped and shrieked. 'He's there! Look, Lucy, he's there!'

'Of course he's there,' said Lucy calmly, although she was far too small to see properly. 'I *knew* he'd be there.'

'Your grandpapa?' enquired a voice beside her.

Kezzie turned. It was Ricardo, standing just behind her.

'I think so.' Kezzie felt her voice tremble.

'You follow me, please,' said Ricardo in his precise English and, picking up her Gladstone bag, he pushed his way through the crowd, making a passage for her and Lucy.

There was a surging mass of people at the exit rail. The crew slung the ropes out, the thick plaits uncoiling across the oily water and onto the quay. The shoremen expertly tied them up.

'This way,' said Ricardo and he took her arm, and guided her to the spot where the gangway was being run out from the side of the boat. He manoeuvred her into a position where she would be among the first to go ashore. Then he handed her back her bag. 'I must go and see to my mother,' he said. 'I will say "*ciao*" but I will call on you some time, if I may?'

Kezzie nodded, and he touched her hair. Then he smiled at her and was gone. She turned back just as the deckhand unhooked the barrier chain.

'Come on, Kezzie.' Lucy's nails dug into her hand. 'Hurry up. I can see Granddad.' She pulled on Kezzie's arm. 'Come on,' she said again. 'We're going home.'

# 4
# Homecoming

And home they came

Lucy raced down the gangplank and, worming her way through the mass of people, she ran at once, with no strangeness or hesitation, into the arms of her granddad He gave a great shout and swung her high up into the air Then, holding her firmly on his hip, he stretched out his free hand to Kezzie.

And it was she who hung back, feeling more grown up and less able to be so free with her emotions than Lucy, her strangeness making it more awkward for her to come forward. Her granddad was looking at her, his head to one side. She was now almost eye to eye with him.

He smiled at her slowly, the lines of his weathered face creasing up in an expression of absolute happiness

'Aye, lass,' he said.

And he came towards her, and kissed her, and then she was just as wild as Lucy had been, hugging him and holding on, never to let go

On the tram out to Dalmuir it was the same Sitting close together. the three of them talking all at the same time. It was only as they walked along the street beside the long line of tenements that eventually Lucy began to slow down By the time they had climbed the first set of stairs in the close where Granddad lived she was beginning to grow weary

'How many more stairs, Granddad?

Lucy's voice was tired and breathless

'We've only come up one flight, hen her granddad

laughed. 'There's lots more to climb.'

Kezzie, several steps behind them, could imagine how her sister must be feeling. She herself was exhausted. Lucy, younger than she and more frail, must be completely worn out.

'Can we stop for a minute?' she called after them, as they reached the second landing.

Her grandfather put the big suitcase down at once. 'I'm sorry, Kezzie,' he said as she caught up with him. He let go Lucy's hand and put both his arms round her. 'I'm just that keen to let ye see the house. I've waited so long for this moment. I'm like a wean, bursting with excitement.'

A door on the landing opened. 'Mr Munro, is it you who is making all the noise?' enquired a very tart voice. 'My husband and son are on nights, and trying to sleep.'

'Oh no,' said Kezzie's granddad quietly. He leaned over and whispered in her ear, 'This one's a real nippy sweetie.'

He took his arm from Kezzie's shoulder. A woman of about fifty stood in the entrance of her house. She had grey hair pulled severely back from her face. A frilled pinny tied at the waist covered her clothes, and she had a duster in her hands.

'Mrs Sweeney,' said Granddad. 'These are my two grandchildren, Kezzie and Lucy.'

The woman glared at them for a moment. 'Aye,' she said. 'I remember ye saying they were due today.' She put her hand in her apron pocket. 'There's a wee bit tablet for the bairn.' She held it out to Lucy. 'I made it myself.'

Lucy hesitated and looked at Kezzie. Kezzie nodded.

'It's all right,' she said. 'It's like the candy you ate back home. Say "thank you".'

'That's very kind of you, Mrs Sweeney,' said Kezzie as Lucy gabbled a hurried thank you and started to pull the wrapping from her sweet. What could Granddad mean by describing their neighbour as sharp and waspish? She seemed very pleasant.

'Don't mention it, dear,' said the older woman. Her inquisitive eyes roved over Kezzie and Lucy, their clothes and luggage. 'The wee one looks as though she needs some fattening up. And,' her eyes flicked up and down Kezzie disapprovingly, 'maybe yersel too.'

Kezzie set her mouth but said nothing. She exchanged a look with her granddad. 'Told you,' his expression was saying.

'Now,' Mrs Sweeney went on, 'we'll have to come to some arrangement about your turn at the wash-house and drying green. I might have to come upstairs and explain it all to you. A young thing like you will have no notion of running a home.'

Kezzie's eyes widened but, with a great effort, she smiled brightly. 'I'll look forward to that,' she replied. 'Meanwhile, please don't let us keep you . . .' she hesitated, and let her eyes rest on the duster in the other woman's hand, ' . . . from any work that you might have to do.' Then she picked up her bag and marched up the next flight of the tenement.

To Kezzie's surprise her granddad was quite gleeful as they continued up the stairs.

'Months and months I've suffered that woman,' he said. 'Every time I'd pass her door, out she'd come, chivvying me about this and that. The sound of my boots on the stairs, muddy footprints on her freshly-washed close.' He laughed. 'You put her gas at a peep, Kezzie. That's the first time I've seen her short of an answer.'

He stopped at last on the top landing.

'Here it is,' he said, and opened the front door proudly.

Kezzie and Lucy followed him inside.

'There's lots of one-room houses in the tenements, they're called single ends,' he explained as he led then through the tiny hall. 'We're a bit better off. It's a room and kitchen, and an inside lavatory. Look.' He opened the first door on the left and proudly displayed the flush toilet with its huge cistern attached to the wall above, and the long dangling chain. 'It'll be very handy in the wintertime, most of the other closes have a shared toilet on each landing. There's a wee glory hole that I'll sleep in. It's really a walk-in cupboard off the kitchen.' He pointed to the door beside the toilet. 'You girls will have this room for yourselves.' He led them inside. There was a bedside cabinet, a wash-stand and a plain single brass bedstead. A little cot stood in the corner. Granddad looked from it to Lucy then back again.

'Oh dear,' he said.

'I'm a big girl now, Granddad,' said Lucy.

'I can see that, hen.' He laughed and scratched his head. 'I spent weeks making that.'

Kezzie put her arm through his. 'Don't worry, Lucy and I will share meantime. It will be more cosy, at any rate.'

They crossed the hall to the main room. The fire was lit in the kitchen grate and the table set for tea. Two easy chairs and a small stool were set around the fire with a big old chest of drawers opposite. Kezzie gazed at it for a moment or two and at the oval mirror above.

'Granddad,' she said, and then found that she couldn't go on. It was the sight of the fire more than anything else that brought back the memories of their life in the miner's rows. The hearth as the heart of the house. Not just for welcome and warmth, but for cooking, and boiling up water to wash and clean. Kezzie felt the tears coming from behind her eyelids. 'Granddad,' she said again.

He came over to her and she put her arms around his neck. He sat her down in one of the chairs. 'You have a wee rest,' he said, and he patted her hand. Then he took out his hanky and blew his nose loudly.

Kezzie wiped her eyes and looked around.

'Some of the furniture . . .' She hesitated. 'It's ours, isn't it?'

'Course it's ours,' said Lucy. 'This is my stool, isn't it, Granddad?' She indicated the stool on which she had sat down.

Her granddad nodded as he stirred up the fire and set the kettle on the grid above the coals. 'I'd kept all the pawn tickets, and I managed to get some of our stuff back. And young Michael Donohoe helped a bit.'

'Michael . . .' Kezzie repeated the name. 'I was thinking of him only last night,' she said. 'Have you seen him recently?'

'He was billeted at Edinburgh Castle for a while, and he used to visit me.' Her granddad paused. 'Your letters, you see . . . I helped him read them. He wasn't very good with the words and he couldn't ask any of his mates. Then the Argylls were posted to Palestine. He went off not so long ago.'

Kezzie felt her heart move within her. She had missed him! She thought of his letters, sent out to her in Canada faithfully each month. The careful elaborate writing. It must have taken him hours to write those few pages. She looked around the kitchen. It was so like Michael to help her grandfather gather up the bits and pieces which they had been forced to sell. She must send him a note of thanks at once.

'How is everyone else?' she asked.

'Yer Aunt Bella's man was laid up again. His lungs are packing in. He's got the black spit, but he's back at work now. She's away to a cousin in the Highlands for a wee holiday wi' the weans.'

'Is the pit on full production?' asked Kezzie.

'Aye, it's the one benefit that war brings. Employment for all. Here, have some tea.' Her granddad was putting milk and sugar into the cups. 'And there's bread and jam.'

He picked up a knife and began to cut the loaf.

Kezzie watched him as he worked He was so much fitter than when she had last seen him The regular pay and the very fact that he was working again showed in his whole demeanour.

She glanced around the room A rag rug would do very nicely in front of the hearth, she thought. She would teach Lucy how to make one. A few cushions would help too, perhaps an embroidered table-cover, and the window curtains . . . They were just what she would have expected her granddad to choose, heavy and dull. Even if they couldn't afford new ones, she would at least make a nice tie-back or fringe the hems.

She looked up. Her grandfather was watching her.

'You're making plans,' he said. 'I can tell. Ye've got that busy look on your face. Your mother was just the same. A few days like that, then the spring cleaning would start or it would be a great round of baking or reorganising the whole house.'

Kezzie smiled. She got up and put her hands around his neck. 'I was only thinking that a few cushions would make the place a bit brighter. You don't mind, Granddad?'

'Mind? Mind?' said the old man. 'I've waited months for this. Each night sitting here on my own. I'd look around me, and well . . . I knew I had a great wee house, but that's all it was, a house. Now you're here, Kezzie, it will be a home.'

# 5
# Settling In

During the next weeks Kezzie and Lucy settled into their new home. To begin with Kezzie noticed every little difference in their living pattern. Instead of the calling of the blue jays from the tall trees in the woods around Waterfoot rousing them in the morning, they awoke to the sounds of the Clyde. The elegant fretwork of the ever-moving cranes, black lace against blue sky, made a backdrop to the constant noise. The ringing, hammering and clatter from shipyards, the tramp of tackety boots in the streets, and the blare of the hooters which ruled the days and the lives of the workers.

Life in the tenement was strange to Kezzie. She had seen tall buildings as she passed through the big Canadian cities such as Montreal. They called them skyscrapers on the other side of the Atlantic. The tenements here weren't nearly so large but she found it odd to live in such close proximity to others and to have to share your garden and washing line. The people in each close seemed to think of themselves as a kind of extended family. The three small boys on the first floor now called Lucy their cousin and looked on Kezzie almost as an aunt. Houses were rarely locked, and in the ones with younger children, the front door lay ajar for most of the day. There was great rivalry between the closes. Mrs Sweeney was the self-appointed leader in Kezzie's and looked down with scorn on the others in the street. She carried tales of their inferior conditions. Their middens were overflowing, their children less well behaved, the stairs and landing not so well kept.

Kezzie had quickly been informed which day was hers at the wash-house and when she could use the drying greens. She tried very hard to be friendly and polite, although she found Mrs Sweeney a great strain.

'I think ye might have won her round,' her granddad told her one evening. 'She almost smiled at me tonight Mind you,' he added, 'it nearly cracked her face to do it.'

Lucy giggled.

'I don't know,' Kezzie sighed. 'She tries to find fault with everything I do. Nothing seems to please her. She thinks I'm far too young to be keeping house.'

There was a sharp rattle at their letterbox and an empty cotton reel dropped through onto the mat. Lucy picked it up and brought it into the kitchen.

'Must be the bairns playing about,' said her granddad. He took it from her. 'But seeing as how it's handy I'll just make ye a wee knitting bobbin.'

Lucy watched fascinated as he hammered in the points of four small nails, one in each corner of the top of the wooden spool. Then he wound some woollen yarn round the nail heads, looping it through so that the tail dropped down the centre hole.

'See?' He took her small fingers in his own and showed her how to do it.

'Ye can make a knitted cord as long as you like, any colour you fancy,' he said.

In a few minutes Lucy was following his instructions.

'What can I use it for?' she asked Kezzie.

Kezzie picked up the end of the thin tube of knitting which was beginning to appear through the end of the cotton reel.

'Lots of things,' she said. 'A hair ribbon maybe, or laces. You can lay it flat, wind it round and round and then stitch it together, and make a hat for your doll.'

Lucy frowned, concentrating hard on her bobbin knitting.

It wasn't until some days later that Kezzie discovered exactly why the cotton reel had been posted through their letterbox. As she returned from the shops Mrs Price from the floor below was standing chatting to Mrs Sweeney on the landing.

'This close is needing a good sweep and scrub if you ask me,' the older woman proclaimed loudly. She shook out her duster vigorously. 'I do my share, and I'm sure you do yours, Mrs Price. It's up to others to do theirs.'

Kezzie put her shopping bag down.

'Would you like me to do it this week?' she asked politely.

*Like* ye to do it,' repeated Mrs Sweeney indignantly. 'I should think so. It *is* your turn.'

Kezzie flushed. 'I'm sorry,' she said, 'I didn't know.'

'Didn't ye no get yer bobbin?' demanded the older woman.

'Bobbin?' repeated Kezzie. 'I'm sorry, I don't understand.'

Mrs Price smiled and laid her hand on Kezzie's arm. 'I put the empty thread spool in your door a couple of nights ago when my week was finished. I thought you'd know what it meant.'

'No,' said Kezzie, looking from one to the other.

'It means it's your turn to do the stairs,' said Mrs Sweeney, 'and when you've done them, you pass the cotton reel on to the next person. Then they know that their turn has come around again.'

'Oh!' said Kezzie. She covered her mouth with her hand. 'We didn't realise . . . Granddad made Lucy a knitting bobbin with it.' She started to laugh.

Mrs Price joined in, and eventually so did Mrs Sweeney.

'I'm so sorry,' said Kezzie. 'I'll do them at once.'

'Don't harass yourself,' said Mrs Price, 'it can wait.' She looked at Mrs Sweeney. 'Why don't you both come down to my house and have some tea?' she said.

Kezzie accepted the offer quickly. Granddad's house was easy to keep clean and tidy, and she found more and more that her days were dragging out. She had resolved that as soon as Lucy began school she would find a job and then see about taking night classes herself. She had not forgotten her dream of one day being a doctor. She had found out that the high school ran evening classes to prepare students for university entrance exams. She had decided that towards the end of the summer she would go along and enrol.

Mrs Price too was lonely. She was fairly young, not long married, and her husband was in the army. He was still based in Scotland, but for how long?

'Robert says the war is only weeks away,' said Mrs Price as she poured the tea. 'He's expecting orders to leave at any moment.' Her hand shook as she picked up the milk jug. 'I might never see him again.'

Mrs Sweeney shook her head. 'Ye'd think after the last time folks would have learnt their lesson. I'm glad my two are firemen. They'll not get called up.'

Kezzie could see the anxiety on Mary Price's face. Her own thoughts were with Michael. She tried to change the subject.

'When Lucy starts school, would anyone come along to the pictures with me?' she asked. 'I've never been to a proper cinema before, and I'd love to see what it's like.'

By chance Kezzie had hit upon the one thing that Mrs Sweeney loved doing. When her husband and son were working nights and had to sleep during the day, then it was a way of passing the time, rather than staying at home and disturbing them. She was an authority on every picture house in the area. She knew the best prices and all the films worth seeing Before Kezzie left to go upstairs and prepare the evening meal they had made a date for her first expedition to La Scala, the local cinema

On the first day of school, as Kezzie was having Lucy enrolled, the teacher spoke to her.

'There's an opportunity to have the little girl evacuated,' she said.

'Where to?' asked Kezzie.

The teacher shrugged. 'We never really know They are sent on trains into the countryside and it's decided when they get there.'

Kezzie felt Lucy's hand tighten on her own

'No, thank you,' Kezzie said pleasantly. 'My sister is staying at home.'

Later in the afternoon when Kezzie collected Lucy from school, the teacher thrust a piece of paper into her hand.

'Here is a list of articles for evacuees to take with them,' she said, 'in case you change your mind.'

That night, after Lucy had gone to bed, Kezzie read the list out to her grandfather.

'"Spare clothing, toothbrush, comb and handkerchief, and a bag of food for the day." And they tie labels around their necks,' Kezzie went on. 'It's as if it's a parcel you are sending away, not a child. I can't believe it's happening.'

'When the war starts it might be safer in the country,' said her grandfather. He looked across the table at her.

Kezzie stared at him. 'What do you mean?' she asked sharply.

He sighed. 'I'm thinking it was very selfish of me to want ye both to come home. It could be that I've put you in danger . . .'

'We had to come back,' Kezzie said firmly. 'It was the right thing to do, not just for you, but for Lucy and myself too.'

'Yes, but,' her granddad persisted, 'it's possible that this area, with the yards and the docks, isn't going to be very safe Perhaps we should think about getting her out of it.'

'Never,' said Kezzie.

Granddad looked at her carefully. 'If the bombers do come . . .' He didn't finish the sentence.

'Never,' said Kezzie again.

There was a soft rustling noise from the kitchen doorway. They both looked up. Lucy was standing there in her pink fleecy nightie.

'Kissy can't sleep,' she said, holding up her doll.

Granddad held out his arms.

'Bring her over here,' he said. He took Lucy and the doll onto the chair beside him. 'I've got a new story for ye.' He poked up the fire and then settled back in his chair. 'A royal story,' he went on mysteriously. 'D'ye want to hear it?'

Lucy nodded.

'Well, coorie doon beside me,' he said, 'and I'll tell you all about it. Did you know that when the work is finished on the hull of a big ocean liner, they launch the boat into the water and then take her away to be fitted out?'

Lucy shook her head.

'Well, that's how it's done. And the one I was working on last year was a very special one indeed. It was the biggest and the best, and when it was finished they asked Queen Elizabeth, the wife of the King, to come and launch her. On that very special day, which was September the twenty-seventh, there I was, walking around John Brown's shipyard, and did I not come face to face with the Queen of Britain herself?

'"John Munro?"' she asks.

'"Aye, that's me,"' I reply.

'"Ye've made a grand job of her," says she, looking the

boat up and down. "They tell me she's the largest liner in the world. I'm fair pleased with you."'

'Your tales are becoming as fanciful as Michael Donohoe's,' Kezzie interrupted.

'It's the gospel,' said her granddad, 'as sure as I'm sitting here.'

Kezzie lifted a handful of peas in the pod from the vegetable rack and put them into a small basin. Her granddad winked at her and went on with his story.

'"Yes," said Queen Elizabeth, "she's a magnificent ship, John. And I'm very happy to be here today."'

'"Thank you very much, Your Majesty", I said. "Now if you'll just excuse me, there's things need doing."'

'And I give her a nod and off I go. And do you know she was so busy chatting to me that she nearly forgot to let the bottle go?'

'Blethers!' said Kezzie.

'It's true,' he protested. 'It's absolutely true. Ask anybody. It was in all the papers.'

Kezzie shook her head and started to shell the peas, as her granddad went on with his story.

'There was a great crack and a groan. The ship had started off down the slipway without anyone realising it! What a panic! But Queen Elizabeth stayed completely calm. She leaned over, quick as she could, snipped the ribbon and let the champagne go. Just in time, she was. The bottle struck the ship on the very tip of her bows as she slid towards the river! What a magnificent sight as she entered the water! What a roar went up! Hundreds and hundreds of people cheering and waving, and the flash and pop of the camera light bulbs. And the rust-red dust from the chains rose up in a great cloud as they dragged along. Everyone flung their caps in the air. It took me three weeks to find mine again!

'And then the Queen catches a glimpse of me, and she

gives a wee wave of her hand. And I can see her telling the two princesses, "That's John Munro, the best shipbuilder on the Clyde."'

When they were sure Lucy was safely asleep, Kezzie and her granddad talked for a little while by the fire. As if by unspoken agreement neither of them mentioned the war.

'I'm going to look for a job now that Lucy's at school,' said Kezzie. 'Remember you wrote to me when I was in Canada saying you might know of somewhere that would fit in with my studying for university?'

'You don't need to go out to work,' he replied. 'With my wage, there's enough coming in for us to manage.'

She smiled at him. 'I know that,' she said. 'But if I do finally get a university place, then I'll need some savings to fall back on.'

He smiled back at her. 'You've still got that inside you?' he asked. 'Ever since you were small, you were determined that you were going to be a doctor.'

She nodded.

'I'll ask tomorrow,' said Granddad. 'It's a wee café, run by Italians.'

'Oh,' said Kezzie. 'I met some Italians on the boat. The Biagi family.'

'This one's called Casella's,' said Granddad, 'though I wouldn't be surprised if they were related. It's a shop and a café, right next to the yard, just off Glasgow Road. I'm friendly with the owner, and I'm sure she could do with some help about the place.'

A few days later, early in the morning, Kezzie went to keep the appointment her grandfather had made for her. As she crossed the street in front of the café she could see through the large glass window fancy chairs and tables with smart red checked covers. Further back was a delicatessen with shelves of cheeses, jars of pasta, and various types of sausages hanging from the ceiling. Standing behind the counter refilling the biscuit tins stood a dark-haired boy. He turned around as Kezzie entered the shop. It took several seconds before Kezzie recognised who it was. The last time she had seen him he had been wearing a formal suit with an elegant bow tie.

'Kezzie!' he cried, and his smile was like the sun coming out.

# 6

# Casella's Café

'Kezzie!'

Ricardo Biagi hurriedly wiped his hands on a cloth and came out from behind the counter. He kissed Kezzie on both cheeks.

'My aunt told me to expect a new assistant today, but I had no idea it would be you! When can you start?'

Kezzie laughed. 'At once if you wish,' she said.

'We are so very busy here,' said Ricardo. 'We serve tea and ices in the café. Many people come from the yards and the workshops. At lunchtime the *garzoni*, the apprentice boys, are sent by their bosses for sandwiches and pies. All day we deliver grocery orders in the van.' He took off his apron and presented it to her. 'You may begin immediately.'

Kezzie found that she enjoyed working in the shop. It was very busy, as Ricardo had said, but it was fun to meet and talk with so many different people. The friendly atmosphere on both sides of the counter compensated for the hard work. Signor Biagi ran the deli, as he called it, ordered the stock and made up the boxes for delivery to houses and institutions. Ricardo's mother and his aunt mainly stayed in the kitchen and cooked, which left Kezzie and Ricardo dealing with the front shop.

Kezzie was intrigued by the vast range of goods on sale. She enjoyed looking at the coloured and patterned labels on some of the boxes and tins, and trying to read them in Italian. Ricardo would spell the words out to her and she repeated them, stumbling over the unfamiliar pronunciation.

He would laugh and hold his head in his hands. 'It's that flat Scottish accent,' he complained. 'It is most unsuited to our melodious language.' The only success she had was when there was an 'r' in the Italian word. Then she would exaggerate the sound and roll it around her tongue to make it sound out.

On the back of the shelves were rows and rows of fancy glass jars with a colourful range of sweets inside. Tiered stands stood in front displaying slices of home-made chocolate cake and fudge set upon fancy lace doilies. There were cartons of ice-cream wafers, bottles of olive oil, hams and salami, and a variety of cheeses. The whole smell of the place, the mingling of cultures, the very signs marked on the goods gave it the exciting feel of an exotic bazaar.

In pride of place above the counter was the large framed photograph of Signor Casella, resplendent in his First World War British Army uniform, proudly displaying his medal and decoration.

After her initial difficulty Kezzie found that she loved the Italian words. The items on sale, cannelloni and mozzarella, and the Italian places such as Umbria and Calabria. Even Ricardo's friends and relatives who called in, usually on a Sunday, had interesting and unusual names; Bruno and Marietta, Serafino and Rosario. There were cousins, uncles, nieces, who came to chat, or have a coffee or a game of cards. Sometimes when the café was full Kezzie's head spun with their language, so rich and vibrant, and their extravagent gestures as they spoke.

'No more!' she would cry eventually, flinging her hands in the air in imitation of Ricardo's mother when she was agitated. 'I give up! I am not serving any more until somebody speaks to me at less than a hundred miles an hour."

She liked the weekday customers too. She responded to the cheeky banter of the shipyard workers, the teasing and open flirting They always noticed if she wore a different blouse, bought a new comb or slide, or altered her hairstyle in any way. And within a few days she knew their special likes and sandwich combinations.

Kezzie and Ricardo worked well together There was an easy friendliness between them And his casual manner, which she perceived as being particularly American, made it less awkward for her when confronted by the many branches of his family.

It was good to have him to talk to. The women that she knew and spoke to in the tenement were all married. She had been to the pictures several times now with Mrs Sweeney, and had soon discovered that the older woman was very lonely With her husband and son's shift pattern she was often on her own. Her son had never married so there were no grandchildren Kezzie realised that Mrs Sweeney looked forward eagerly to their weekly outings, and although Kezzie enjoyed her visits to the cinema with Mrs Sweeney, she still missed company of her own age She had enrolled for the night classes but found that it was mostly older men who attended. One of the tutors had made enquiries for her as to the appropriate subjects to study, and she was taking maths and Latin classes. These were not popular subjects with younger women.

Also, she discovered that she had a unique bond with Ricardo in the strange unsettled feelings which tormented her from time to time.

Sometimes she felt a longing for Canada that she could not explain even to herself, far less talk it over with Granddad. Lucy seemed to have had little difficulty in readjusting to her life in Scotland. She was a favourite with adults and popular with her playmates. She had adapted to school life very well, although she was teased sometimes about her accent and the names she used for everyday things, referring to motor cars as automobiles and biscuits as cookies. But it was good-natured and some of the children in the close now called their toffee bars and sweets 'candy' as a joke.

It wasn't like that for Kezzie. Occasionally she stood at the tenement window and gazed down into the street. She could see the children playing with hoops and balls. The boys with marbles and bogies and the girls skipping, the rhythmic chant of their song keeping time with the slap of the rope on the pavement. It was all so friendly, homely and yet . . . *different*. In many ways childhood games were the same all over the world, but all the little particular things varied. Yet this was what she had been used to most of her life, and what she had longed to be back among, when she was away. So why now did this place, this home, seem strange? Why did she sometimes feel alien to the everyday happenings here?

It was comforting to know that Ricardo's thoughts were similar. The lack of space, he told her, was what had scared him most in the beginning. He was used to the wide freeways, the low bungalows set back from the sidewalks, acres and acres of parking lots, four- or six-lane highways.

He saw the gritty grey buildings here closing in on him. The width of the streets was so narrow in places that housewives in the upper storeys had strung washing lines across. The sky and clouds seemed closer, as if you could reach and touch them. In America, and in Canada also, she told him, the space seemed endless, stretching out and up into infinity.

They spoke about it often, and about the whole problem of adjusting.

Kezzie thought it must have been such a shock for Ricardo's grandfather who had come so long ago to Scotland, and exchanged the clear sunny skies and the heat of Italy for this mild and wet climate.

'Perhaps we are not so dissimilar, though,' Ricardo had

said 'The family is important here, and so it is with Italians We stay together, we look out for each other '

They spent much of their spare time together, and it seemed a natural thing for him to hold her hand as they strolled along the road or through the park One evening on their way home from the pictures as they stood chatting under the lamp post at the end of the street, he bent down and kissed her on the mouth After a moment he raised his head

'You enjoyed that, no?'

'Yes,' Kezzie replied 'It was very pleasant.'

He smiled at her, a soft sad smile..

'Pleasant,' he said ruefully, 'is not what I intended it to be.'

He took her arm and continued to walk her home. She felt she had let him down in some way, but didn't quite know how.

The topic of conversation everywhere was the disturbances in Europe. How long could it go on before Britain was drawn in? Kezzie knew that the Italian families in Clydebank were worried about their position should war break out. In the First World War Italy and Britain had been on the same side, but a few months ago Mussolini had allied himself with Hitler and Germany. Each day the newspapers were full of events and political discussions. Ricardo's parents were now not sure whether all three of them would be better off returning to America, or staying on for a while in Britain. There were rumours of German submarines patrolling the Clyde coast.

'We had no idea things had reached such a state here,' Signor Biagi told Kezzie one day. 'Where we lived in the States, we did not hear much foreign news. Most Americans will not be aware of what is happening over here.'

For the time being the Biagis decided that they would stay.

Kezzie had received a reply from Michael. He felt as badly as she did to know that she had returned to Britain and he had missed her.

*I will desert immediately*, he wrote, *and will sail all the way back across the sea. Please stand by the pier at Greenock and look out for a small boat and a very seasick soldier.*

She smiled as she read this extravagant declaration. She knew that there was a fine thread of seriousness in it. She also knew that she herself felt inclined to some similar reckless act so that they could be together.

As she walked to the shop each day it seemed to Kezzie that the mood of the town was changing. Shop windows were taped up, a precaution against flying glass in the event of an air raid. People seemed anxious, and every shop or street corner had someone speculating on exactly what would happen. Sitting in the back green one Sunday, near the end of August, she heard a group of men, of whom her granddad was one, talking together.

'I don't think *we* need tae worry aboot air raids,' said Bill Forbes, who lived in the next close. 'These big bombers they've got could only be used short range. They're far too heavy to stay up in the air for long.'

Kezzie heard her granddad laughing.

'Aye, they said something the same about the *Queen Elizabeth* when we were building her. That she'd be far too heavy to stay afloat.' He tapped the hot ashes out of his pipe. 'She hasn't sunk yet,' he said.

'Well,' said another, 'Scotland's too far away for their fuel to last out. London might get it, but anywhere from the north of England up should be all right.'

'You're reckoning that they would always be travellin' fae Germany,' said Mrs Sweeney's husband. 'Supposin' they came in fae Denmark or Norway?'

'Norway!' repeated Mr Forbes. 'Whit the hell would the Germans want wae Norway or Denmark?'

'I think Herr Hitler wants everything he can take,' said Kezzie's granddad quietly.

'I still think their fuel tanks won't be big enough,' Mr Forbes persisted. 'What with the weight of the bombs, and the size of the planes and the number of crew and equipment needed, they wouldnae hae enough fuel tae get here.'

'They'll have enough tae get here,' said Mrs Sweeney's husband. 'Aye, tae get here *and* get back.'

Mr Forbes shook his head. 'Ye'll be sayin' next that folk will be journeying as far away as the moon,' he said.

Everybody laughed at this. Kezzie looked across. She noticed that her granddad wasn't smiling.

She worried again about Lucy. Perhaps it was best to make some arrangements for her? To get her out of this area? If there were aerial bombardments she knew that Granddad believed that the shipyard would be a target. Should she have taken the chance to evacuate Lucy? Kezzie resolved that, as soon as her Aunt Bella returned home, she would go and visit her and discuss the matter with her.

Meanwhile Europe and the world held its breath and waited.

The last few days of August and the hot summer of 1939 dwindled. On the first day of September German forces invaded Poland. Two days later, on a Sunday morning, Britain declared itself at war with Germany.

# 7
# War!

'Well, that's us now, isn't it?' said Mrs Sweeney grimly as Kezzie passed her on the stairs the next day. 'Anither war. In my lifetime too.' She shook some Brasso onto her cleaning cloth. 'They promised when the last one finished that it widnae happen again.'

Kezzie stopped on the landing and watched her neighbour determinedly polishing the already gleaming letter-box on her front door. It suddenly struck her that Mrs Sweeney was frightened. As scared as most people were, but trying not to show it.

Kezzie reached out and touched her arm. 'It'll be all right,' she said. 'We'll manage . . . somehow.'

'You dinnae ken what it was like,' said Mrs Sweeney. 'You young ones, you dinnae ken.' She shook her head, and Kezzie could see that there were tears in her eyes.

Kezzie walked more slowly downstairs and along the streets of Clydebank. Every newsagent's had the headlines displayed outside.

BRITAIN AT WAR<br>TIME RUNS OUT<br>WAR DECLARED

As she approached the café she could see that the blinds were still drawn. Inside the shop, Ricardo, his parents and his aunt were sitting at one of the tables. The two women were holding each other and weeping. Kezzie said nothing but went straight to the kitchen and put the big coffee pot on the stove. The thought of war scared her too. Her grandfather had fought in the Great War. He rarely spoke about it except to say that it had been a waste of young life. She knew that many of his friends had been killed. They had marched away, he had told her once, hundreds and hundreds of them, thinking it would be exciting and glorious, whole villages joining the same regiment. Then when the big battles were fought sometimes not one boy from a village survived. They came home singly, or in twos and threes, often badly mutilated.

Kezzie made some sandwiches, then poured out four strong cupfuls of coffee with plenty of sugar and took it through to them.

'Eat something,' she ordered. 'Things aren't as bad as they seem.'

'For us,' said Signor Biagi gravely, 'it could be quite serious. The authorities might try to take the café from us, or put us in prison.'

'What!' cried Kezzie. 'Why would they do that?'

The Italians looked at each other. Eventually Ricardo's mother spoke. 'We are not British citizens,' she said. 'None of us have British passports.'

'But I don't think the United States will fight against Britain in this war,' said Kezzie. 'You will be quite safe with your American passports.'

Ricardo's mother and his aunt exchanged fearful glances. 'Our passports are Italian. Even Ricardo does not have full citizenship.'

'It shouldn't be such a big problem.' Kezzie tried to make her voice sound reassuring. 'Signora Casella, your son is British. He'll be fighting in the British Army.' She pointed to the picture hanging on the wall of the café. 'Your husband won a medal in the last war.'

Ricardo spoke up. Kezzie realised that he too was trying to calm his parents.

'Kezzie is right,' he said. 'There is nothing to fear. We have done nothing wrong. We will mind our own business and people will leave us alone.'

A few Sundays later Kezzie was to remember his words.

She had asked for some time off and set out early in the morning to visit Aunt Bella. As the ancient single-decker bus wheezed its way through the countryside towards Stonevale, Lucy's excitement was indescribable. She seemed to remember everything: the burn where she had fished for tadpoles, the hills they had climbed when berrying, the canal bridge where the horses had to wait until the gatekeeper swung back the heavy wooden barrier to let the coal scows through.

They lurched over the bridge and Kezzie, catching sight of the long barges, suddenly recalled the Sunday School trip of two summers ago when their father had still been alive. It had been the last outing which they had enjoyed together before he was killed in the pit. It was in her mind now. All of it. The smell of the mown grass in the field where they held the races, the taste of the lemonade, the long gloaming as they glided home along the calm water of the canal. Kezzie saw the scene in front of her blur and dissolve, and raised her hands to wipe her eyes. Suddenly, small fingers were intertwined with her own. She looked down at Lucy, who smiled bravely back at her.

Had the child sensed her grief and was trying to give her comfort? Kezzie gripped her sister's hand tightly.

They came closer to their own village and, as they passed each place and Lucy called out in delight and chattered about some incident which had happened in her past, Kezzie was amazed at how early some of her memories were.

'Are you quite sure you really remember what happened that day?' she quizzed her sister on one occasion.

Lucy was adamant. She could tell Kezzie the colour of

the dress she had been wearing and whether Kezzie had been cross with her for something she had done wrong. Kezzie watched her in wonderment. She looked at the little face framed with the fine blonde waves. Her sister's hair was longer now, less baby-soft, and tended not to curl so much, but it still settled round the child's face in an angelic cloud. And as her sister became happier and gayer as they came near the little mining village where they had both been born, Kezzie knew with utter conviction that she had done the right thing in bringing her back from Canada.

It was a circle closing. A last link that had to be made to connect Lucy's life now with that of her previous one, to give her some coherence, make some sense of her childhood which had been so cruelly disrupted. And as they walked up the road together towards the miners' rows it felt to Kezzie that she herself had completed some kind of particular and significant journey. The air itself, full of the sounds and smells of her homeland, was in her mouth and hair, and then, quite distinctly, in her very being. And like the exile returning, she was suddenly, and to her own surprise, in tears.

Lucy had run on, unannounced, straight into her aunt's house, and Bella came rushing out, tying on her apron, and flung herself at Kezzie. And they were both laughing and crying and trying to tell each other everything at once. But they found that it was not all tears of sorrow that they shared as they sat together and reminisced about the last years. They spoke of the fun of the annual day trip in the summer, and Kezzie told Bella about Canada, and Bella in turn brought her up to date with local news. Her children now were almost as tall as she was, and still as cheeky. But Will, the eldest, was determined to get a foundry or ironworks apprenticeship rather than go down the mine. He was working hard at school and the teacher was giving him instruction in technical drawing.

'Most folks are workin' now,' said Bella. 'There's nothin' good about a war at all, except that it brings employment.'

At the mention of the war Kezzie told Bella about her fears for Lucy.

'I don't know whether we would be attacked, living so far north,' said Kezzie. 'Granddad seems to think so. I'm not sure what's the best thing to do. If she was sent away again, it might distress her too much. Aunt Bella, at one stage in Canada, she was so ill that she didn't know where, or even who she was.'

'Leave her here wi' me,' said Bella at once.

Kezzie thought this typical of Bella's generosity. Her house was already overcrowded, and her husband working less and less as his lungs became weaker and weaker.

At that moment, Lucy, in the middle of some game, came running past the side of the house where Bella and Kezzie were sitting. Bella called her over.

'Ye like yer Aunty Bella, don't ye, Lucy?' she said.

Lucy nodded.

'Then would ye bide here wi' me, pet, for a holiday?' asked Bella.

'No,' said Lucy at once.

Bella laughed out loud.

'Well, that's a straight answer anyway,' she said to Kezzie. She turned back to Lucy. 'Aw, c'mon,' she wheedled, 'Just for a wee while, eh?'

'No,' repeated Lucy. She went and stood beside Kezzie. 'We stay together.' She looked directly at Kezzie. 'You said, didn't you, Kezzie?' she asked her sister. 'You told the teacher at school, I was staying at home.'

'So I did,' said Kezzie, 'so I did.' She drew the child to her and wrapped her arms around her. Through a blur of tears she looked at Bella over the top of Lucy's head.

Bella smiled at her.

'What has to be, has to be,' she said.

As she was about leave, Kezzie suddenly remembered something else she had wanted to ask.

'Do you ever get any news of Peg?' she asked

'Which Peg?' said Bella.

'Peg McKinnon,' said Kezzie 'Her dad and one of her brothers were killed at the same time as . . .' Kezzie hesitated. She glanced to where Lucy was playing a few yards away . . . 'as Daddy,' she finished softly. How great the pain had been at the time, she thought The whole small community crushed by that blow. And yet Granddad and Bella, who had counselled her wisely, had been proved right in the end. Remember the good things and resist bitterness, they had said, and then all your memories will be happy ones. Kezzie heaved a great sigh It was difficult, and especially difficult now, in the shadow of the pit itself, right beside their former home.

Bella reached over and gripped her hand tightly

'We were friends at school,' Kezzie went on 'I often wonder what happened to her. The family left the village right after the accident. I think they moved to either Glasgow or Clydebank. She said she would write to me but she never did. I'd love to see her again.'

Bella looked away. 'I heard . . .' She stopped

'What?' said Kezzie 'What did you hear?'

'That . . . that they were in a bit o' bother The mother died. An' the brother . . .' Bella's voice tailed off again

'Aunt Bella,' said Kezzie in exasperation, 'please tell me. I'm not a child any more that you have to keep bad news from me.'

'No, I suppose ye're not,' said Bella slowly 'Ye had to grow up gey fast, hadn't ye, hen?' She sighed 'The brother's married and has a wean Or maybe has a wean and is no' married. Who kens? Anyway, he's taken to drink The woman . . . is . . .' Bella spread her hands out in front of her and examined them carefully for a moment or two She heaved a sigh 'They say she goes with men all sorts of men, even brings them tae the house '

'And Peg still lives there?' asked Kezzie in horror

'I think she's nae option but tae,' said Bella There's naebody else cares aboot the bairn '

There were geese settling beside the small loch as the bus taking Lucy and Kezzie back to Glasgow turned on to the main road Breaking formation as they approached the water, the birds flapped and squawked as they made their ungainly landing The sight of them reminded Kezzie of Canada and the great long lines of migrating birds which had filled the skies in spring and autumn Kezzie smiled as she recalled the sight, a happy relaxed smile She was more at peace now with herself She felt altered in some way by her visit to her home village She knew that, since her travels, her perspective had changed Like the pit ponies returning to the surface and having their blinkers gradually taken off, she was now looking at everything in a new way But her unease was wearing off Instead of being upset and withdrawing into herself, like some nervous tortoise, she decided she would now look forward and welcome new experiences Perhaps if more people could travel and meet each other, as she had done, then there would be less prejudice, fewer wars Folk would appreciate what they had, as Ricardo had said, they would see the similarities which united them

In Glasgow Kezzie and Lucy got off the country bus and boarded a tram They were going to go directly to the Casellas café It was too late now to go and look up Peg's address, which Aunt Bella had given her, and she had promised that she would spend some time clearing up in the shop this evening, and preparing food for tomorrow, in exchange for her time off today Dusk was quietly closing in as Kezzie and Lucy dismounted at the tram stop in Glasgow Road They hurried along quickly With the new blackout regulations there was little light, apart from that which came from the sun, slowly setting beyond the Mull of Kintyre As they turned down the street where the café was located, there was the sound of running feet. heavy shoes and boots clattering on the cobbles And voices calling, rudely yelling and shouting, with screaming and crying in the distance Kezzie pulled Lucy into the nearest close mouth as a crowd of people rushed past her

'Wait here,' she instructed Lucy

The shop was no more than a hundred yards or so away, and it was with a terrible sense of dread that Kezzie ran towards it.

There were staves of wood and pieces of fencing lying in the roadway A half brick, some stones and pieces of rubble were scattered on the pavement And everywhere broken glass Great pieces of the ornate glass door. on which the name Casella had been proudly etched in fine script, lay in the gutter The large front window was splattered in mud Beyond that, in the shop itself, the tables and chairs had been smashed or overturned Kezzie came to a halt, her whole being struck with shock The lace curtain, now in tatters, flapped at her helplessly She could now see clearly what had happened

The café had been completely wrecked

# 8

# The Café is Wrecked

Kezzie picked Lucy up and carried her over the shattered glass and in through the café door Signora Casella was sobbing noisily in a corner, her face buried in her apron She was being comforted by her sister Signor Biagi had a small cut on the side of his face which his son was cleaning with his handkerchief

'What has happened?' Kezzie asked

Ricardo's face was pale under his tan

'We were attacked by a mob,' he said Kezzie, I am glad you were not here We have been insulted, dirt smeared on the windows, people calling us filthy names My mother,' his voice broke, 'my mother was spat on as she walked to church this morning '

Kezzie gasped

'Did you not inform the police?' she asked

He shook his head What can they do? It is happening all over Britain Since the Aliens Order came into force, requiring all Italian nationals to register with the authorities, we have been a focus of hatred and fear We are seen as the enemy '

'The enemy!' Kezzie repeated The enemy! You are almost American ' She pointed to the framed photograph on the wall behind the counter Your uncle won medals in the last war fighting for the British!'

'I know, I know ' Ricardo picked up a chair which had been kicked over and sat down wearily But I couldn't reason with them It was terrible They were gathered outside when I came to open at lunchtime Some had been drinking It was very ugly.'

'Did you recognise anyone?' asked Kezzie 'Were there people that you knew?'

Ricardo looked away.

'Perhaps,' he said evasively

'You must tell the police,' said Kezzie

'No,' said Signor Biagi

Ricardo also shook his head

'No, Kezzie,' he said 'That would only make it worse, much worse.'

Signor Biagi went to the back shop and returned with a broom He began sweeping the broken glass.

Lucy crossed over to where Signora Casella sat She stood, uncertain and afraid, at the sight of adults crying so loudly.

'Would you like some tea?' she asked after a moment

Signora Biagi looked up 'What a wonderful idea, Lucy I'll come and help you'

'No,' said Lucy 'I can manage' And she went through to the kitchen.

Kezzie looked at the destruction about her At the once beautiful glass jars, now lying in pieces on the counter and the floor Stones and bricks had been hurled at them The toffees and fudge and all the cakes were ruined and would have to be thrown away One of the pretty little tables was broken beyond repair

A feeling of panic was growing inside her If the newspaper reports were true then this was what was happening to the Jews in Germany The hounding and persecution of people because they were of a particular race And ordinary folk were being manipulated to do this Their fears and worries exploited, their raw emotions stirred up and whipped into a frenzy of violence against their fellow humans, and all because they were of different origins It was obvious to Kezzie by the expression on

Ricardo's face that he had known some of the mob. Perhaps there had even been customers among them.

She recalled something which had occurred in her early days of working in the café. Two girls of around Ricardo's age had come in, and they had obviously been very taken with his dark good looks and his charming manners. Very soon they were flirting with him and ordered another ice-cream each. When he brought it to their table, with much whispering and giggling they had demanded to know his name.

Kezzie watched as he smiled his wonderful smile. She could not help smiling herself at their teasing, or indeed overhearing the conversation.

'My name is Ricardo Biagi,' he said.

They made him repeat it until they themselves could say it properly, imitating his pronunciation, his way of making the words sound so lilting and musical. Then they protested that it was too tricky, too difficult for them to remember.

'Why don't you change it?' suggested one girl. 'The way it is just now, it sounds too Italian.'

'But I *am* Italian.'

'Yes,' said the other, 'we know you are. But you could easily alter your first name. Why don't you just make it Richard, instead of Ricardo?'

Kezzie stopped what she was doing and lifted her head to watch Ricardo's face. He took a step back from the café table.

'I am Ricardo,' he had replied proudly, 'Ricardo Biagi. *Not* Richard. My parents chose this name especially for me, and I do not intend to change it.'

He smiled at them to show that there was no bad feeling on his part. 'How can I be something I am not?' he asked 'I am an Italian. An Italian who is called Ricardo.'

Kezzie looked at him now, slumped dejectedly in the

chair, and at the two women almost hysterical with fear. It was quite possible that they would not be able to keep the café going any more.

A sudden anger filled her mind How dare people do this to them? Ricardo and his family worked so hard. They cooked and prepared food each day, and kept their little café spotlessly clean. Kezzie looked again at the mess and confusion, and her eye fastened on the photograph of Signor Casella, resplendent in his British Army uniform Kezzie stared at it for a long moment

Lucy had cleared a table and was very carefully setting out teacups. Signor Biagi was sweeping the glass into a pile.

Kezzie went over and took the broom from him 'Leave it,' she said.

'Such a mess,' he replied 'We have to tidy up.'

'No,' said Kezzie firmly. She raised her voice and spoke to all of them. 'I want you to leave everything exactly as it is.' She turned to Ricardo 'Ask your aunt if she still has your uncle's medal and ribbon which he won when he was in the army, and if she has, may I borrow it? And see if she has a photograph of your cousin in his uniform.'

Without waiting for a reply Kezzie dragged one of the café tables over to the counter and climbed on top She lifted down the picture of Signor Casella from its place of honour.

'Now,' she said, 'we will board up the door so that the place is safe from thieves tonight, and tomorrow we will open for business as usual.'

Signora Biagi opened her mouth to speak Kezzie raised her hand.

'Listen,' she said 'We are going to humiliate these people They will expect you to be cowed and frightened, or angry and vengeful We will be neither '

She took the ribbon and medal from Signora Casella and

draped it carefully over her husband's picture Then she placed it on a table with the photograph of his son in uniform beside him. She tore the remaining piece of lace curtain from the window and set the table in the centre, facing out into the street.

'There,' she said. 'Now let them all look at that as they go about their business tomorrow, and as they do so let them also see the brave thank you that the family of those who fight for Britain receive.'

The next morning Kezzie asked Mary Price to take Lucy to school and she herself went to the café very early She worked with Ricardo and his family to clear up only what was required in order to make the sandwiches and the snacks for the usual orders They left the overturned chairs and tables and the pile of broken glass in the corner. The stones and bricks which had been thrown lay where they had fallen

And they didn't complain about the situation to anyone Ricardo and Kezzie kept smiling as they served their customers, and Kezzie found as the morning progressed that more and more people found it difficult to meet her gaze She knew that anyone who entered the café had to pass by the two photographs on display

Just before lunch-time a policeman came into the shop He walked to the front of the line of people waiting to be served Then he took out his notebook and nodded to the mess by the window.

'Who did this?' he asked Ricardo

'I saw no one,' said Ricardo firmly

'Ye must have seen somebody, son,' said the policeman reasonably He turned to Kezzie 'Explain it to him, Kezzie,' he said 'If he can give us a name, we can mebbe do somebody for it '

Kezzie laughed 'Ricardo understands perfectly,' she said 'What he is trying to tell you ' Kezzie looked at the queue of customers still waiting to be served She raised her voice 'What Ricardo is saying is that he truly believes that no person that he knows, or has ever met, or who buys food in his café would ever do something so horrible to his family '

The policeman closed his book 'Suit yerself,' he said

There was silence in the shop as Kezzie and Ricardo dealt with the remaining apprentice boys and the factory orders Kezzie determinedly kept up a stream of conversation making jokes, teasing and calling after them as they left Around half past two, when the shop had gone quiet, Ricardo leaned wearily on the counter

'I don't know how you managed to keep chatting all the time,' he said.

Kezzie handed him a tiny cup of the black expresso coffee which he so loved

'I was rather enjoying myself,' she said mischievously Did you notice that there were very few customers who could look me straight in the face? Those who weren't involved probably have a good idea of who was, and most folk will be ashamed and embarrassed at what has happened here '

As she spoke the café door was suddenly thrown back Two young men in their working clothes stood just inside One of them spoke 'My boss says he wants this door '

'What for?' said Kezzie

'Needs fixin', don't it?' said the other He took a large screwdriver from his pocket and began to unscrew the hinges.

Ricardo made to come out from behind the counter Kezzie pulled his sleeve

'Leave them,' she whispered

Half an hour later, the door was brought back reglazed In the meantime a few more lads had drifted in They began to pick up the broken pieces of glass and crockery, and straighten the chairs and tables A young woman who lived opposite the café brought over a long piece of white netting. She attached it to the window curtain-pole and hung it back in place All afternoon this went on, neighbours bringing little gifts and staying to help By early evening closing time Signora Casella was in tears She flung her arms around Kezzie.

'*Grazie, grazie.*' She kissed her effusively

Ricardo put his hands on her shoulders

'You are so very clever, Kezzie,' he said What you did has not only resulted in many of our broken things being replaced. It has also given us a place in the community '

'Remember, Kezzie,' said Signor Biagi, 'if we can ever do anything to repay you, we shall do it '

Kezzie went home that evening with a comforting warm feeling inside her Her trust in others and human goodness had won through today She didn't realise how soon it would be that she herself would be asking the Biagi family for help.

# 9
# Peg McKinnon

The streets where Kezzie now found herself were mean and dirty. She had walked north on Kilbowie Road, away from the river for nearly twenty minutes, and then turned off to the right. She took out the slip of paper on which Bella had written Peg McKinnon's address. There was no mistake. Slessor Street, past Drumry.

It was the correct road that she had turned down a few minutes ago. Kezzie looked around her and sighed. She remembered the neat little houses of the village where they had both been raised. The scrubbed and whitewashed steps; the lines of washing strung out to catch the wind. Peg's mother had struggled to keep their two rooms clean. With three working miners in their family it was a constant round of washing and drying clothes, a labour of love, particularly troublesome in the winter time.

There was something more depressing about the poorer parts of cities, thought Kezzie. When Granddad, Lucy and herself were near starvation in the little bothy at least there had been clean air about them.

The atmosphere around these particular tenements was grey and damp. There was rubbish lying in the gutters, empty beer bottles and horse dung. The grimy window panes were broken and the curtains grubby. The appearance of these houses suggested that no one cared.

Or perhaps deep, unrelenting poverty did this, thought Kezzie. Constant unemployment, where hope had long since left the hearts of the people caught in this situation, and they found that they turned in circles until their energy was gone.

Kezzie stopped at the entrance where the number she was seeking was written in faded copperplate on the wall. She mounted the inside stairs warily, peering at the doors in the dim light. She smiled to herself. Mrs Sweeney would have a fit if she saw the state of this particular close.

'Middle floor left.' Kezzie read the instructions on her note.

The door in front of her had no name or number on it. It needed repair and a coat of paint, but the handle and surrounds had been washed down and the little mat, although worn, was clean. Kezzie knocked firmly on the wooden panelling. From inside she heard a baby begin to cry. Someone yelled out, 'Shut that wean up, can't you? I'm trying to sleep.'

The door swung open violently. A man stood there. He was swaying on his feet.

'What d'ye want?' he demanded roughly.

'Johnnie?' said Kezzie. She took a step back in order to see him better. 'It is Johnnie McKinnon, isn't it?' She smiled at him, overcome with an unexpected feeling of affection. Despite his aggressive manner and his unshaven face, she recognised him immediately. Where Peg's hair was golden like her dad's, he favoured his mother, with thick carroty red curls. And his voice too placed him at once. He hadn't lost the country lilt, the soft vowel sounds which were at odds with the flatter tones of the city.

'Johnnie,' laughed Kezzie, 'don't tell me you don't know me. After all the times you pushed me off the top of the coal bings!'

He narrowed his eyes and said gruffly, 'Who are you?'

'Kezzie Munro. You used to pull my hair and tease me until I cried.' And without being able to help herself Kezzie reached up and kissed him on the cheek. They had strong links of friendship, the McKinnons and the

Munros. Having no brother herself, it had been Peg's two brothers who looked out for Kezzie in childhood scraps. They had all grown up together, Peg and she sharing everything: their secrets, life at school and at home, and eventually death too. Kezzie's father had died beside Peg's in the local mine. Peg's other brother had perished in the same disaster.

'Come away in.' Johnnie McKinnon grabbed Kezzie's arm and shouting out loud, he pulled her into the house. 'Look who is here after all these months! Peg! Look who has come to visit us!'

Peg McKinnon was sitting by the fireside, holding her brother's baby on her lap. The little boy was gurgling happily as she crooned to him and stroked his back. She turned and placed him in his crib and stood up to greet Kezzie.

Again Kezzie felt this great rush of love and fondness, and she could see that Peg was experiencing the same. The two girls hugged each other for several minutes.

'Gosh, Kezzie,' said Peg at last, 'you are so much taller and browner. Canada must have treated you well. I'd heard of your trouble with Lucy, and I'm sorry I never tried to get in touch.' She shook her head. 'But our circumstances are such that we can hardly get by ourselves, far less help anyone else.'

'Yes,' said Kezzie awkwardly as they sat down. 'I heard things weren't very good for you.'

Peg wiped her hand wearily across her face, tucking some hair back behind her ears. 'I remember reading a newspaper notice at the time Daddy and Sandy were killed,' she said. 'It gave details of the fall at Stonevale pit. "Not a major disaster" were the words they used. Well, it was for us. That one accident killed not only my father and one brother,' Peg sighed. 'It also killed my mother. She just pined away. And it's ruined Johnnie's life.' She glanced at the door of the room where her brother had gone to lie down again. 'He can't stay away from the drink.'

Kezzie looked at her friend. She wasn't many months older than Kezzie herself but her face had an altogether sadder set to it, her big eyes grey and melancholy, her soft mouth turned down.

Kezzie glanced around the kitchen. Despite her friend's best efforts, the room was drab and bare. Kezzie guessed that most of their possessions had gone the same road as her own once had. Pawning household goods and personal belongings became a way of life for many people struggling to live.

'Have you tried to look for work?' she asked Peg. 'It would get you out of here for a bit, and bring in some money.'

'I'm terrified to leave baby Alec for any length of time.' Peg lowered her voice. 'Johnnie's wife ... she doesn't always come home, and when she does she often brings drinking friends. I don't think she feeds him properly. And ... I think she hits him sometimes.'

Suddenly Peg started to weep. Kezzie put her hands around her friend's shoulders. She was thinking furiously. 'I may know a place where you can get a few hours' work,' she said. 'And we'll figure out something for the baby. There are these new crèches and day nurseries now for mothers who are working to help the war effort.'

Kezzie decided to go straight back to the café and ask them to employ Peg. She wondered if Mary Price, who sometimes collected Lucy from school, would mind the baby. Mary seemed to enjoy any company, and Peg could give her a few shillings from her wages. Knowing how much the Italians loved children, perhaps Peg could even bring the baby with her to the café. Called for his grandfather, baby Alec seemed to be a contented wee soul. She would check with Ricardo. They knew that they could do with some extra help in the café, even another pair of hands to wash the dishes would be of use.

When she returned to the café she found Ricardo in the tiny back garden He was erecting an Anderson shelter He had already dug a large hole and had set in the end wall and the side pieces of curved corrugated steel She watched him as he bolted them together at the top and then began to shovel earth on the roof. They said it could withstand a five-hundred pound bomb going off less than fifty feet away.

Kezzie tried to imagine what it would be like, a whole family crouching down in the small space for hours on end, listening for the all-clear to sound Would they hear the noise of the dropping bombs, as they sat there with their gas masks on, wondering and waiting, without knowing what was happening above them?

Lucy and Signora Biagi came out of the back door of the café. Ricardo's mother shuddered 'Please God we never have to use that I'm too old to stoop down to get in there '

Kezzie smiled as she thought of Signora Biagi, who was always so perfectly turned out, hurrying to the shelter in the middle of the night.

Lucy was waiting impatiently for Ricardo to complete his work She already had cushions and an assortment of books and toys ready to furnish the shelter

'I think it'll be great fun,' she said

Signora Biagi smiled sadly and murmured, Such are the days now that children think of war as fun '

As she had guessed, Ricardo and his aunt readily agreed to employ 'Kezzie's friend What Kezzie had not anticipated was how apprehensive Peg was about the prospect of going out to work again She brushed and redid her hair several times and complained to Kezzie about the state of her clothes

'Look,' she wailed, pointing to her elbow 'I've darned this cardigan twice already, and the wool doesn't even match properly '

'Nonsense,' said Kezzie firmly 'Everyone is doing the same now Mending and patching things Only the other day I cut down one of Granddad s shirts, worn at the collar and cuffs, to make a perfectly good nightie for Lucy '

They approached the café from the other side of the road Kezzie could see Ricardo leaning on the counter reading a newspaper which he had spread out in front of him Beside him his father was packing boxes

Peg dragged Kezzie to a stop 'I'm so nervous,' she said She fiddled with her hair for a moment and adjusted the belt of her coat.

'You look trig,' said Kezzie

And she was being truthful Peg had long legs and her coat with its cinched in waist showed off her slim figure She had pleated her dark golden hair into a single plait which hung over one shoulder, and had pulled her beret down on the other side

'Very smart,' Kezzie repeated, and propelled her across the street

Kezzie was right behind her as they entered the shop so she did not see Peg's expression when her friend first caught sight of Ricardo But she did see Ricardo's face quite clearly He glanced up as the café door opened He recognised Kezzie, had been expecting her in fact, but was so engrossed in his newspaper that his eyes flicked away from her again, back to study the article he was interested in Kezzie saw his head start to bend . . and then stop

Ricardo looked back at once to the two girls, but it wasn't Kezzie he was staring at It was Peg Peg who had his whole attention

Signor Biagi also had witnessed the scene He followed

his son's gaze to the young woman who stood just inside their café Then he turned his head and gazed fondly at his son He clicked his tongue between his teeth, and Kezzie heard him say something in Italian

*'Colpo di fulmine!* he murmured

# 10

# Love at First Sight

Kezzie looked at Peg, then she looked at Ricardo. Her friend's cheeks were flushed pink and Ricardo's usual radiant smile was not in evidence. His face was very solemn.

'We have met before, I think,' he said to Peg.

Peg stared at him without replying. Kezzie nudged her.

'What?' Peg turned to Kezzie.

'It isn't me that's speaking to you, Peg,' said Kezzie. 'Ricardo is asking you if you've met him before.'

'I . . .' Peg hesitated. 'I don't think so,' she said eventually.

'No?' said Ricardo. 'I was so sure . . .'

He stared very hard at Peg's face. In return she lowered her head and then glanced at him sideways.

'I don't think we've met,' she murmured.

Kezzie regarded the two of them in amusement. They could hardly drag their gaze away from each other, yet didn't seem able to conduct a coherent conversation.

'I'm going through to the kitchen to make some fresh coffee,' she said loudly.

Neither of them appeared to hear her.

'*Un colpo di fulmine*,' Ricardo's father said again as he followed Kezzie into the kitchen.

'I can say *buona sera* and I know what *ciao* means,' Kezzie laughed, 'but *colpo di* whatever is too much for me.'

Signor Biagi made a gesture with his arm and placed his hand theatrically on his chest. 'It means a thunderbolt. Struck by lightening Just here,' and he pointed to where his heart would be. 'Love at first sight is the translation you might use. And there is no cure,' he added. He opened the kitchen door a crack and peeked through. Then he turned to Kezzie and winked at her. 'Nor would it seem that those who are thus afflicted wish there to be,' he said

Peg's nephew was an immediate hit with Ricardo and his family. They had agreed that Peg could bring him along for the few hours she worked each day, and he thrived in their warm loving care. Signora Casella found her own son's high chair from when he was a baby, and Alec would sit, propped up with pillows, watching everything that happened in the kitchen. Lucy adored him and he would turn his head at the sound of her voice when she sometimes dropped in on her way home from school in the afternoons

Kezzie wondered about his natural mother.

'Doesn't she miss him at all?' she asked Peg one day

Peg wiped a dribble of food from the baby's chin. 'I don't think she notices that he's not there,' she said 'Johnnie shows him more affection than she does '

The café shut earlier now in the winter months Custom had fallen off in the evening anyway and the streets were much quieter at night. There had been so many road accidents that the blackout regulations had been relaxed slightly. People were allowed a small torch with a dim light when walking home after dark, and the shop van could use lights if they were properly shaded White lines were painted on kerbs, tree trunks and lampposts

Everyone had a gas mask, in case the enemy dropped containers of poison gas Even baby Alec had a Mickey Mouse one. He hated it and used to yell and scream when Peg tried it on him.

'There, there.' Ricardo picked him up and cradled him in his arms He rested the small golden head on his shoulder and walked up and down for a few minutes, rocking the little boy gently and crooning to him in Italian

'You have no idea at all how to treat a baby? Do you?' he scolded Peg

'Of course I have!' she replied indignantly 'I've taken care of him since he was born

Ricardo placed his finger on his lips 'Shh!' he said severely 'You mustn't raise your voice It will alarm the child This boy and I have a great *simpatico* We are not well treated by Miss Peg McKinnon All we require is a small amount of affection, and do we receive this? Do we?' He pretended to ask the now sleeping child, then he shook his own head sadly. 'No, we do not.'

Peg looked at him, her face going pink

Ricardo's eyes gleamed 'Just a tiny piece of kindness occasionally would do,' he went on 'A fond look, a sweet smile, perhaps, would make us so very happy '

Kezzie saw Ricardo hand the sleeping tot back to Peg and she smiled up at him His hand brushed Peg's bare arm and she blushed As she watched them flirting with each other, Kezzie suddenly thought of Michael Donohoe and a terrible loneliness came over her He had written again and she had replied at once But it wasn't the same Nor anything like it.

She didn't know whether to be glad that Michael's battalion was in the Middle East and not on mainland Europe The Argyll and Sutherland 51st had now gone off to France There was talk that they were guarding the Maginot Line, and would be the first to see action, yet the weeks went by and nothing much seemed to be happening People had relaxed to such an extent that many of the children who had been evacuated all over Britain came home again

At the end of that year, and the beginning of 1940, it was as if Christmas came twice for Lucy and baby Alec

The Italians celebrated the visit of the three kings on January 6th. So, in addition to having Santa Claus bringing presents to their own homes, the two children also had the Befana, or the good witch, who brought gifts to well behaved children. Little packets of sugared almonds and pieces of marzipan cake were hidden around the café for Lucy to find.

The very same month the Government decided to ration some food items, and, as sugar was one of the first chosen, it wasn't long before the café had to stop selling ice-cream. It only made a small difference to the café's business, but many Italians, who sold mainly ice-cream, were badly affected. Kezzie knew that Ricardo and his family were worried, not only from the commercial side, in that supplies were becoming difficult to obtain, but also the political aspect of the war frightened them. Mussolini was obviously prepared to collude with Hitler in his territorial ambitions. What position would they be in if Italy openly allied itself to Germany? The war had seeped in to all parts of ordinary existence. Everywhere now people were in uniform, of one kind or another, or rushing to join the volunteer services. Granddad was firewatching most nights, and Peg and Ricardo went to first aid classes. Everybody wanted to help, 'to do their bit'.

In the early spring Kezzie received a letter postmarked Derby in England. It was from William James Fitzwilliam, the young man she had become friendly with when she had been on her way out to Canada to search for Lucy. He told her that he had been accepted by the RAF. He finished his letter with the words 'If Douglas Bader can do it, then so can I.'

He was referring to his leg which had muscle deterioration below the knee. The doctors he had consulted in America had given him exercises and therapy to try to stop the wasting process. Kezzie wondered about his mother, and how she felt about him enlisting in the armed forces. He would be sure to see active service against the Luftwaffe, who were a powerful and skilled fighting unit When Kezzie had met the Fitzwilliams on the boat crossing the Atlantic to Canada, Lady Fitzwilliam had barely been able to let William out of her sight No doubt she felt it a great honour for him to be in the Air Force

And then the war news became more grim.

In April German troops invaded Denmark and Norway A few weeks later they overran Belgium and Holland The main body of troops, including the Highland Regiment were sent forward to halt the enemy advance through the forest of Ardennes The German Army proved unstoppable By the end of May, the British Expeditionary Force had been driven back to the sea on the northern coast of mainland Europe They were exhausted, outnumbered, and completely encircled In and around the small French town of Dunkirk they were fighting for their lives.

Signor Biagi turned the knob on their wireless set The voice of the broadcaster crackled through from London, sending out the call for the little boats to come and bring the soldiers home And they responded, streaming out from every port, all the South Coast, and from further north they came. river cruisers, fishing smacks, anything that could float

'This is crazy,' said one of the apprentice boys standing at the counter 'These are ordinary sailors they are asking to do this, they are civilians Some of their boats are no bigger than dinghies You can't expect them to go over there and face shells and bombs just to pick up half a dozen men.'

'They'll have to get them off any road they can,' said Kezzie's granddad, who was in the café 'That's the most experienced troops we've got We can't let them be rounded up '

They all looked at each other, each one with their own thoughts. It could be Michael, Robert Price, Signora Casella's son, and any one of all the rest, brothers, lovers, husbands, fathers, waiting on the shoreline to be rescued. Being pounded by artillery and rifle fire, hoping that help would arrive.

Kezzie's granddad sighed heavily 'We're taking a beating today. Now their U-boats will control the Channel We might have to fight an invasion . . . The only thing that stands between us and them now are the boys in the Air Force.'

In the next weeks Britain waited . . . and prepared itself. The Home Guard was formed and 250,000 men volunteered for this citizen's army On Kezzie's last visit to Bella all the road signs had been removed No church bells were to be rung The country knew that when next they heard the peal of bells it would signal that the enemy had arrived.

Just after Dunkirk, on the 11th of June, Mussolini declared war on the Allies One late afternoon when Kezzie was at home ironing, there came a tremendous pounding on the front door She ran quickly to open it Peg stood there Her hair was wildly uncombed and her face was streaked with tears

'The police,' she gasped, out of breath with running so quickly upstairs 'The police and some military men . . . In the café—' Her voice was shaking and she was on the verge of hysteria She grabbed Kezzie by the front of her dress

'Kezzie,' she sobbed, 'you have to come at once They've arrested Ricardo and his father!'

# 11
# 1940: Internment

When the two girls reached the café it was shut and in complete darkness. They knocked on the door and rattled the window but no one answered. Kezzie went through the pen at the side and round to the back entrance. She banged on the service door.

'Signora Casella! Signora Biagi!' she called loudly. 'It's Kezzie and Peg. Let us in!'

Several minutes elapsed and then the door was cautiously pulled open a crack. Such fear on their faces made Kezzie shiver. Alec was squirming in their arms as they clutched him desperately. They had expected men with guns, thought Kezzie, as she followed them upstairs into the house.

The two women were beyond tears.

'The *combattenti*,' Signora Biagi told Kezzie. 'They took my son away.' She kept repeating, more to herself than anyone else, 'We have done nothing wrong. We have done nothing wrong.'

Kezzie and Peg looked at each other helplessly. They sat down round the big circular table. Signora Casella twisted the hem of the embroidered cloth over and over in her fingers. She turned her large brown eyes on Kezzie. 'My sister and I, we are scared to go out on the street. What can we do? What will happen now?' she asked.

Kezzie shook her head. 'I don't know. First of all we have to find out what is going on.' She stood up. 'I'll go to the police station and see if I can get any information. I'm sure it's all a terrible mistake.'

Half an hour later Kezzie discovered that it was not.

'Sending them away?' She repeated the words the desk sergeant had just said. 'All the Italian men living in Britain? Where are they being sent?'

The sergeant shrugged his shoulders. 'I don't know. They're setting up camps in different places.'

'Camps?' said Kezzie sharply. 'What kind of camps?'

He hesitated before replying. 'Like detention camps, sort of,' he said 'They'll be all right,' he went on. 'It's just a precaution.'

'You mean camps such as they have in Europe?' demanded Kezzie. 'The same as the Nazis have done. Those people that we are fighting against.' She heard her own voice rising higher and higher. 'One of the reasons we are at war, in fact?'

The policeman fidgeted under her gaze. 'Don't take on so, hen. It's not as bad as you think. They'll get treated quite well.'

Kezzie took a deep breath. 'Where are these places?' she asked quietly. 'And where are the Biagis just now?'

The sergeant consulted some papers. 'I can't give you exact information,' he said. 'They could be on their way to one of the islands. There's also been talk of shipping them out to Canada or Australia for the duration. Come back tomorrow and ask again.'

As Kezzie hurried back to the café her thoughts were swarming in confusion. The policeman had said 'the duration'. Did he mean the whole of the war? How long would that be? And what could she tell Signoras Casella and Biagi? Or for that matter Peg, who was completely distraught about Ricardo.

She felt desperately sorry as she gave them her news.

Peg was stunned. 'I didn't know they could do things like that in Britain,' she said.

'When there is a war, they can do anything they please,'

said Signora Casella.

Despite the restrictions on reporting, the newspapers carried the story over the next days. The entire Italian male population of Britain between the ages of seventeen and sixty had been rounded up. There was a large Italian community in the west of Scotland and many of Signora Casella's friends and relatives were involved. Eventually they discovered that Ricardo and his father were part of a group who had been kept at Maryhill Barracks and then sent on to the Isle of Man. Their cases would be reviewed in time, meanwhile the family could apply for permission to visit, though it would not be for many weeks.

'This is awful,' cried Peg. 'How can we afford to travel all that way to see them? How can we take the time away from the shop?'

'The shop,' said Signora Casella. 'How are we going to manage the shop? How are we going to survive?'

Her complaint was echoed in a thousand other households. The internment had struck a blow into the very hearts of the Italian families. Worse was to follow.

One of the ships transporting some of the men to detention in Canada was torpedoed and sunk. Only hours after its departure from Liverpool the *Arandora Star* was attacked by a German U-Boat and over four hundred Italian men were drowned.

A great gloom settled over the shop No cooking was done or food prepared. Kezzie found that she missed the smells of the frying oil, and the baking dough, the constant flow of the Italian conversation. She and Peg stacked the café chairs and tables to one side, and only sold the grocery goods. Custom began to fall off. It was a sad place to be, and even Lucy, coming in from school, swinging her legs from one of the high bar stools commented on it.

'There's no happy noises in this café any more.'

Kezzie realised it was true. The wireless was only switched on for the news bulletins, and Peg and herself hardly spoke as they served behind the counter in the deli. Occasionally Kezzie could hear one or other of the older women breaking out in a heart-rending lamentation Peg wasn't much better, wandering around listlessly, beginning a task and not completing it Baby Alec quickly picked up the mood of the place and became grizzly and fractious Their supplies were running low. Kezzie saw that if they did not reorder soon the shop would have to close She called them all together one morning and told them that she had made a decision.

'We are reopening the café tomorrow,' she announced.

Signora Biagi shook her head sadly. 'Not without the men,' she said.

'Yes,' said Kezzie firmly. 'Lots of other women are doing it, working in factories and on the land while their men are away. They can manage, so can we. Also I hear that there are tribunals we can appeal to. There is a very good chance that they might be released early, particularly Ricardo. His citizenship papers were almost cleared.'

'I cannot cope with it any more,' said Signora Casella.

'Do you want your own son to come home from the war to no business?' demanded Kezzie. 'If we don't begin our sandwiches and lunchtime snacks again soon then we will lose all our customers.' She appealed to Peg for help. 'We can run the front, can't we?' she asked.

'Yes, probably,' said Peg. 'I suppose we owe it to them to keep going.'

'We've got to try, at least,' said Kezzie. 'It's not doing us any good moping all the time. Look at you,' she spoke to Signora Biagi. 'You who were always so neatly dressed, with your hair so beautifully arranged. What a welcome for your husband should he return just at this moment.'

Signora Biagi glanced in the mirror hanging on the

wall. She sighed and fixed one or two hair grips in place.

'Kezzie is right,' she said 'We must at least try.'

'So.' Kezzie rubbed her hands together. 'Tonight you make some pasta. We will share all our ration coupons and make some chocolate cake and pies And then we will begin again.'

# 12
# Kezzie Learns to Drive

To begin with it was really Lucy and the baby who kept them going. Alec was teething and demanded constant attention. With the shortage of teachers Lucy was attending school only in the mornings and she spent most of the afternoon in the café helping out. She was alternately petted or scolded, depending on the prevailing mood in the kitchen. She was becoming an expert in pasta making, mixing and beating the flour and egg and water, rolling it out and cutting and folding the special shapes. Her favourite was ravioli, and Signora Biagi had taken much time to demonstrate exactly how to press and flute the ends together.

Kezzie watched her sister working so carefully and seriously, looking up every so often to check with Signora Biagi that what she was doing was correct.

'Is this enough?' she would ask, her hand holding the flour shaker above the pastry board. She would wait until one of the signoras would nod their head before continuing.

And Kezzie noticed that she didn't shirk the unpleasant or difficult tasks. Lucy would wait until the dishes were done or the surfaces scrubbed before untying her apron and saying, 'I think it's time for some tea.' Everyone had laughed on the first occasion Lucy had come out with this expression. But now, despite her youth, she was rapidly becoming one of the work team in the kitchen.

Ricardo and his father wrote frequently. Their letters were amusing and light-hearted. Kezzie was sure that they guessed how anxious Signora Casella and Signora Biagi would be and deliberately filled the pages with remarks about their seaside vacation and the wonderful bed and breakfasts which they enjoyed. Many passages were blocked out by the censor but they had been held at a temporary camp in Wales before being sent on to the Isle of Man. There they were put in what had been holiday hotels, and the accommodation, although cramped, was bearable. They had fared much better than some of the others who were sent to Canada and Australia, and kept in what were no more than prisoner-of-war camps.

At home there was a frightened tenseness in conversations with neighbours and friends which Kezzie had never been aware of before. The bravado and old-style jingoism had disappeared. People kissed and embraced each other more obviously when parting even for a short time, and what was more unusual, they did so in public.

The new Home Guard trained and drilled regularly. At first the butt of many jokes with their ludicrous and out-of-date equipment, more and more people realised that these men might have to make the last stand before the enemy. Many veterans of the First World War had enlisted, men older than her grandfather.

'If they do land, they'll find it harder to beat us than they expect,' said one old man sipping his weak tea in the café. 'We'll fight to the bitter end.'

It was a mood which seemed to prevail through the whole country. Listening to a recording of the Prime Minister's speech one evening on the radio gave Kezzie an eerie feeling. The slow drawl, the hesitant slur of the words coming from the squat wooden box set on its shelf in the corner of the counter. Churchill's voice, giving hope to millions of people.

*'We shall defend our island, whatever the cost may be, we shall fight on the beaches, we shall fight on the landing grounds, we*

*shall fight in the fields and in the streets, we shall fight in the hills: we shall never surrender.*'

In the café they kept the business going, and drafted Mary Price in to help wash dishes and mind the children.

'It's giving me something to take my mind off worrying about Robert,' she told Kezzie, 'and I love playing with the wee ones.'

She had had some news from her husband. In the retreat his battalion had reached Cherbourg, and had finally been safely evacuated to England. There was talk of the rescued troops being sent to open up a new front in the East or in Africa. Or were they in fact preparing to fight on British soil?

Mary was an energetic worker and a cheerful soul. She tuned the radio station to *Music While You Work* and sang along with the current hits. She had taught Lucy all the words. Their favourites at the moment were the songs from the Disney version of *Snow White*. They sang together, to the amusement of the customers, while Mary danced around the kitchen with the baby on one arm and Lucy holding on to the other.

She's like a child herself, thought Kezzie. And even though Mary was older than her and married, Kezzie felt that in some ways she was more mature. The days of the summer of 1940 slipped away, each one told off like beads on a prayer circlet. Counted out singly, every sunset and sunrise a bonus of peace as the country braced itself for the expected invasion. Special buses and trains took the children away from the south coast of England far inland. Some of them had been evacuated previously from the larger cities. And above their heads in the long hot summer the RAF was fighting a desperate battle for control of the skies over Britain.

Carefully worded letters from William James made Kezzie realise that he was part of it. His mother now had also taken to writing to Kezzie. Her letters showed how proud she was of him, yet her anxiety and worry lifted off the very page as Kezzie read them. She tried to reply to each one as best she could.

Day by day the invasion seemed imminent. By August over a thousand enemy planes were sent on sorties daily into Britain. How long could the RAF keep them at bay?

Then on the seventh of September the Luftwaffe broke through the defences of Fighter Command and set London ablaze.

Kezzie's granddad scanned the papers. 'They're not telling us the half of it,' he said.

Night after night they kept coming. The Londoners fled to the underground stations, carrying bedding, children, food and water. It was a city under siege from the sky. And in the mornings the Londoners came out of the darkness and looked upon the devastation of their homes.

Lady Fitzwilliam wrote to her.

*Kezzie, the bombing continues. They will not stop, neither will they go away. Our boys will fight until they die, each and every one of them, yet the safety of our children concerns me deeply. I sense and know that you would not like to lose sight of Lucy, nor she of you, for even a short time. I suggest that you both come and stay with me. I am far out in the country and it would be as safe here as anywhere else. Please give the matter some thought. I already have some children billeted here, so it would be no trouble to me. Also, I would appreciate your company, as would William, that is if he ever does get any leave.*

Kezzie didn't show the letter to anyone. She knew that at the moment she was needed in the café. It was taking her full attention and, as the days passed, the finances became more grave. By not delivering the large orders which they had done before, they were starting to lose money. One day Kezzie asked Ricardo's aunt for the keys and went out to the wooden lean-to where the van was garaged.

'It can't be *so* difficult,' she said, assuming a great air of confidence. She took the keys quickly from Signora Casella's hand. 'I've watched Ricardo lots of times when he was driving.'

She sat in the van and turned the key in the ignition. The engine roared and the van leapt forwards and smacked against the wooden wall of the garage.

'Ooops,' said Kezzie.

'There's something about gears,' she told Peg when she returned to the café later. 'I think that bit of it is quite important. If I could just get someone to explain it to me, I'm sure I could pick it up fairly quickly.'

She tried to coax one of the apprentice boys to give her a lesson.

'Nae chance.' He shook his head. 'Women can't drive. They're not built for it.'

'Nonsense,' said Kezzie. 'I think you're scared,' she said, attempting to goad him.

He grinned at her. 'Aye, ye're right there, hen,' he said. 'I'd rather face the Jerries than get behind a wheel wi' you.'

Kezzie put her hands on her hips. 'There must be some way I can persuade you,' she said. She stared at him boldly. 'Something I could give you, perhaps?'

'Aye . . .' he said slowly. He looked her up and down. 'I'll tell ye what ye could gie me . . .' He broke off.

Kezzie snapped her fingers. 'I know,' she said. 'My sugar ration!'

'Yes,' said Peg from the other end of the counter. 'You can have mine too. And my butter as well.'

'And mine,' volunteered Lucy, who had come through from the kitchen without anyone realising it.

'I . . . I . . .' the boy stuttered. 'I didnae mean that.'

'And what did you mean, exactly?' asked Kezzie, hands on her hips again.

'Oh nothin',' he mumbled.

And so his fate was sealed. Kezzie's first lesson was the very next afternoon.

'How do I stop it?' she asked, after a few minutes, turning round in her seat.

'Put yer foot on the brake!' he yelled. He made a grab for the steering wheel. 'And keep yer eyes on the road!'

'You didn't show me the brake to begin with,' said Kezzie later when they had returned to the café.

He sat down in the nearest chair, took his cap off and, pulling a hanky from his pocket, he wiped his face.

'How was your driving?' asked Peg.

'It's quite easy actually,' said Kezzie. 'I don't know what all the fuss is about. The Government is thinking of introducing tests and examinations before you can get a certificate. I can't imagine why. A child could do it.'

'Give me coffee,' said her instructor. 'An' make it black and strong,' he added.

The bombing of London continued. By the end of September over seven thousand civilians had been killed by enemy action.

'They won't stop coming, will they?' Kezzie asked her granddad one night after listening to the latest broadcast. 'And there's not much we can do about it, is there?'

'If our night fighters can't keep holding them off . . . then we're defenceless,' said Granddad.

'You think they'll come north?' she asked him.

He raised his head and Kezzie saw that his eyes were shadowed. She realised that he didn't want to cause her distress, but he thought that she needed to know the truth.

'Aye, lass,' he said slowly. 'They'll come. And soon.'

# 13
# Lucy Runs Away

Granddad's words were on Kezzie's mind that night. She knew that if she gave the matter any thought at all, then it was obvious that this part of Britain would be a target. Clydebank was a shipbuilding town, known all over the world. John Brown's yards were famed for boatbuilding, both commercial and naval. Warships and troop transportations were slipping in and out of the Clyde ports all the time. Ships from some of the other navies belonging to their allies, such as Poland and Belgium, were repaired or refitted here.

In addition to the yards, there were many other types of production plants clustered around the Clyde. Light and heavy engineering and armaments supplies, the Rolls-Royce works at Hillington and Beardmore's heavy armour plate. When you looked across the central belt of Scotland then the amount of industry concentrated in this one area was immense: from the huge Singer factory and timber yards to smaller units making parts for engines and automobiles. The works ran on from Glasgow City, down the great river and all along the estuary.

One or two enemy spotter planes had flown over, keeping well out of range of the anti-aircraft guns. Everybody reckoned that they must be taking aerial photographs, surveying weather conditions and gathering information to report to their own intelligence units. Probably recording the position of the docks and the layout of the surrounding works, perhaps noting the big oil terminals at Kilmarnock. And no matter what precautions the Government took, such as removing all directional signs, or even the more complicated manoeuvres of installing street lights among the surrounding hills which were empty of people, they could never obliterate one feature: the Clyde. On the darkest nights it glittered like a thick silver cord, twisting, fat and slow, among the tenements and houses spread all around it. And all these ingenious schemes to divert and fool the enemy could not disguise the location of the sea to the river, and the river to the town.

Even young children knew the names of all the aircraft. Spitfires and Hurricanes, Heinkels and Junkers. To them it was exciting and interesting to spot a plane and try to identify it. There were great arguments about the respective fire power and merits of each kind of machine. It was, of course, a huge game that adults were playing and not to be taken too seriously. Lucy would climb on top of the Anderson shelter in the garden at the back of the café and pretend to drop bombs on baby Alec sitting up in his pram, and he would shriek with laughter.

'Play a nice game now, *piccola*,' Signora Casella would plead with her. 'Come, and I will cut some paper dolls for you to dress.'

Ricardo's mother hated hearing the news bulletins. She would cover her ears with her fingers when the broadcasts began.

Peg had laughed. 'You're an ostrich, Signora,' she said. 'Pretending it isn't happening won't make the war go away.'

Was that what *she* was doing, thought Kezzie, as she lay with Lucy cuddled up beside her. Was she burying her head in the sand?

Lucy turned in the bed, and Kezzie adjusted her position so that there was more room. Her sister slept the sleep of the innocent child. Her body heavy, her breathing regular.

What should she do? Kezzie tried to think through her problem logically. She had a complete conviction that if Lucy was sent away again it would have a dreadful impact on her.

And myself, thought Kezzie suddenly. I would hardly be able to bear it. And what of Granddad? The previous separation had torn the little family apart. Perhaps it was selfishness then. She lay considering this for several minutes and while she did so, her sister shifted yet again and, muttering something, stretched out her arm on the pillow. What was she dreaming of? Kezzie wondered. The room was so dark with the blackout blinds on the windows that she could not see Lucy's face. What was she thinking of, her little sister, as she slept on through the night? Lucy's trust in Kezzie was absolute, believing that she knew what was best for her. But now Kezzie was tormented. If she made a wrong decision it could mean the difference of life or death for Lucy.

Kezzie turned once more in the bed, leaning on her elbow as she thought about her own life. Her great aspiration to study medicine seemed almost a self-centred indulgence compared to the war being fought. Yet she knew that it was the right course for her, had known it since she was very young. Her missionary zeal had faded a little, the desire to travel to foreign lands and do good was something she now realised might not be fulfilled. But her determination to qualify as a doctor had not altered. She thought then of Michael. How he had encouraged her ambitions. Their lives, so far apart at the moment, were joined by a fine link which was unbreakable. She wondered what he was doing at this very moment. Was he thinking of her? Kezzie slept at last, and smiled as she dreamed.

The Blitzkrieg continued. Almost nightly, bombs were dropping on London, and then other industrial cities and ports. Daily radio news bulletins and newspaper headlines told of great destruction and death. Docklands and industrial targets were pounded again and again. Then on the 14th of November over four hundred planes attacked the city of Coventry, dropping nearly a thousand incendiary bombs.

Kezzie stopped at the local shop and stared for a long moment at the pictures of the shell of Coventry Cathedral. Its centre had been annihilated in the space of a few hours. The remaining latticed windows and small elongated spires were etched in monochrome relief against the sky. There were people photographed in the streets, wandering about dazed and stupefied, clutching a few possessions, and children sitting amongst the rubble.

Kezzie bought some newspapers and hurried back to their house. Her granddad had come in from night-firewatching and was eating his breakfast. She spread the newspapers out on the table in front of him.

'I'm taking her to Aunt Bella's today,' she said.

He didn't say anything at all. Only stared straight ahead and nodded. When Kezzie returned in the early afternoon he was still sitting at the table. The fire had gone out and he had not rekindled it. The room was very cold.

'I had to get her away from here,' said Kezzie as she took her coat off and hung it up on the peg at the back of the door.

Her grandfather looked up at her. 'You did it for the best,' he said.

Kezzie sat down at the table opposite him. She put her head in her hands. 'But is it?' she asked him. 'Is it for the best? I don't know.'

'I'm surprised that she stayed,' he said after a bit.

'I tricked her,' said Kezzie wearily. 'I told her I was going to the shop, and then caught the bus back to Glasgow from the end of the road. I couldn't even say goodbye properly in case she suspected something.' She put her teacup down unsteadily 'Bella said she'd tell her after a few hours '

'Poor Bella,' said Granddad

About half-past four their letterbox rattled loudly and Granddad went to answer the door Bella came rushing through to the kitchen

'It's Lucy!' she cried 'She's run away!'

# 14

# Ricardo Returns

Bella's coat was flapping open, showing that she still had her apron on, Her face was without powder, her hair falling down.

'Kezzie, John, I'm sorry. I'm sorry.' She looked wildly from one to the other. 'Kezzie, she kept askin' where you were, and what was keepin' you. Ah kept puttin' her off like, with wee stories an' givin' her things to dae. An' then another wifie who'd gone down the road after you, came back up, an' I saw Lucy speaking to her. An' then the wean came over the road, an' she said tae me, awful quiet-like, "Aunty Bella, Kezzie's gone home without me, hasn't she?"

'I just nodded. Ah couldnae say the words. An' what a look she gied me, Kezzie.' Bella put her hands to her face. 'I ken now how Judas felt. But she never complained, nor cried. Nothin'. Only asked me if she could play outside for a wee while.' Bella sat down heavily. 'An' me bein' that stupid, an' that glad that she was takin' it so well, says, "Aye, on ye go, hen." An' then half an hour later when I went to fetch her in . . . .' Bella pulled a handkerchief from her pocket and wiped her eyes.

'Have ye told the police?' asked Kezzie's granddad.

Bella shook her head. 'No,' she said. 'I came straight here.'

'Where d'ye think she'd go, Kezzie?' her granddad asked.

Kezzie couldn't think at all. She realised now that she should never have left her sister like that, in such a cowardly fashion But it would have been too much for her to cope with if Lucy had cried or become hysterical when she told her that she was returning to Clydebank without her

'I don't know,' she said dully.

Granddad made some tea, and as they drank it they talked over what to do.

'I'll go to the police station,' he said 'Then I'll walk the road back to Stonevale '

Kezzie looked at him. He seemed to have aged tremendously in the last few hours It was as though his two grandchildren were the life force which sustained him Now he was drained and barely able to function.

'Yes,' she said. She got up slowly. What should she do now? Her great dread was that Lucy would lapse into the almost catatonic state she had been in when she had gone missing before. When she and Kezzie had been separated previously the shock had been so great for Lucy that she had been unable to tell anyone her name, or where she lived.

Kezzie walked to the window. It was almost dark. Mindful of the blackout regulations, she started to draw the curtains before she lit the gaslight. She stood at the window for a moment and looked out into the night. Where was Lucy? If she was running away where would she go? Kezzie frowned. A memory returned to her, faint yet insistent, of herself standing at a window . . . watching, waiting . . .

Now she recalled what it was. In the McMaths' house in Waterfoot, she had stood looking out into the Canadian wilderness, anxious for news of Lucy's friend, the boy Jack, who had absconded from the orphanage where Lucy had been placed. 'Where does a runaway child go?' she had asked.

'To where they would be welcome. To people who show

love and kindness ' Doctor McMath's words slipped into Kezzie's mind. She turned from the window.

'I think I'll take a walk along to the café,' she said. 'Bella, will you wait here?'

Kezzie hurried through the blacked-out streets, feeling along the brick walls, stumbling off kerbs and hesitantly seeking her way across the roads. She tried to block her mind from the fact that somewhere Lucy might be doing the same. By the time she arrived the café was closed, but Ricardo's mother and his aunt sat with her, in the dark with the door left open, just in case . . .

They made coffee and drank it, and to pass the time they told Kezzie stories of their childhood in Italy. The little farm in the hills of Umbria where they played with the goats in the summer-time. Of how their father had walked all the way through France and England to Scotland, to find work. He had been helped by a *Padrone*, a man from the adjoining village who had already established his business in Gourock and sent for young men and women from his community to work in his shops. Their father had worked hard, they told Kezzie, and when his elder daughter was married he was able to help her and her husband buy this café as a wedding gift.

Despite Signor Biagi's protests they listened to the news bulletins. There had been another raid on London in the early evening.

Signora Casella shook her head. 'The Londoners suffer so much,' she murmured. 'I hope we can bear it so well when it is our turn.'

Signora Biagi shuddered. 'The very thought of that Anderson shelter makes my skin crawl,' she said.

'I don't know if it is so awful,' Kezzie said reassuringly. 'Ricardo made it very cosy, with a rug and some cushions and a lamp. It is just like a little house. Lucy loves to play in it . . .'

Her eyes widened and she gripped Signora Biagi's arm.

'The Anderson shelter,' she whispered.

It was Signora Biagi who restrained Kezzie when they opened the door. Lucy had the oil lamp lit, and was quietly reading a book with the rag doll propped beside her.

'Lucy!' Kezzie screamed and stepped forward. Signora Biagi held on to her arm. 'Do you know the trouble and worry you have given everyone? You are a wicked child to do this.' Kezzie found she was shaking with rage and fear.

'No, I'm not,' said Lucy. 'You lied to me. It was you who caused the fuss. We agreed that I was to stay at home. You changed your mind, and you didn't even tell me.'

'What could I say?' Kezzie asked Peg the next day. 'She was speaking the truth, and was also rather proud of herself that she had found her way there without getting lost.'

'Is your mind more settled now about her staying in the town?' Peg asked Kezzie.

Kezzie laughed. 'Well, I suppose it has to be. She has told me that she'll just run away if I try to evacuate her, so I don't really have any choice.'

But still Kezzie couldn't help but worry. At the beginning of December three thousand incendiary bombs were dropped on the city of London in one night. It was the worst raid ever.

The Chief Fire Officer at Surrey Docks called desperately for help. 'The whole bloody world's on fire,' his signal read.

And it seemed as if his words were true. A red flame-coloured cloud two miles high hung over the capital. The press referred to it as 'Black Saturday'. The fires were out of control and burned for days. The picture of the outline of the dome of St Paul's ascending through the pall of smoke disturbed Kezzie greatly.

Peg took the newspaper gently from her hand.

'When there's nothing you can do about something, then you must try to stop worrying about it,' she said She put her arm around her friend's shoulder 'How do you think I cope with Ricardo being away? It's awful. We don't really know if he and his father are keeping well on the Isle of Man, but I force myself to stay cheerful, for his mother and aunt's sake.'

And Bella also tried to cheer Kezzie up.

'Listen tae me, hen,' she had said on Kezzie's last visit. 'Who kens what's going tae happen? It's all in the hands of the Almighty. I read in the paper yesterday. There was a woman living right out in the country, in Fife, I think it was. Ah mean if yer going to be safe anywhere, it's Fife. Nothin' ever happens in Fife. Nothin'. Anyway, she'd just scrubbed her front step, an' whit happens? A stray plane goin' home jettisons its bombs. Blew her tae kingdom come.'

Kezzie nodded. 'I heard that story. The pilots have to unload their bombs or they don't have enough fuel to get back. It was a tragedy.'

'You're tellin' me,' said Bella. 'All that work tae get yer step clean, an' some bliddy wee Jerry comes along and messes it all up, just like that.'

An appeal had gone out by the Red Cross for relief ambulance drivers. There were few women who could drive and most of the men who could had been called up or were in essential occupations. Kezzie volunteered at once. At last there was some war work which reflected her interest in medical care. She already had first-aid training but, due to the staff shortages, the drivers were often expected to know and do a bit more. Driving the ambulance was even more difficult than driving the delivery van. It was heavier and more awkward on corners and Kezzie took a lot of teasing from the men at the depot. She was given a uniform and a cap, of which she was very proud. She had only bumped it three times, she told Peg proudly, and just once with a patient in it.

Just before Christmas the door of the café opened and a tall young man with a sallow complexion and a thin face stepped inside. He closed the door quietly behind him, and standing with his back against the glass he looked around him slowly.

Peg was refilling the biscuit tins with her back to the counter. She was managing mostly with one hand as she had Alec propped up on her shoulder, and was talking nonsense to him as she worked. The baby, facing the street, suddenly let out a crow of delight. Peg turned round, screamed and then burst into tears.

Kezzie came running from the kitchen. 'What is it? What's wrong?'

Ricardo was at the counter with tears running down his face, his arms around both Peg and Alec. The little boy looked from one to the other and then started howling.

'For goodness sake,' said Kezzie, half-crying herself. 'You're distressing that baby. Here, give him to me.' And she pushed Peg and Ricardo ahead of her into the kitchen. Within minutes everyone was in tears. Kezzie ran through to the front and turned the 'Closed' notice to face out.

Ricardo was disinclined to talk about the camp. His passport had been cleared by the American Embassy and his father had insisted that Ricardo return to Clydebank without him.

'Father is well and sends his love,' Ricardo told his mother. 'He hopes to get out soon but perhaps he will not be allowed to return here immediately.'

His mother covered her face with her hands.

'You must be brave,' said Ricardo. 'They are releasing those who will help with the war effort, working in some industry or perhaps taking part in bomb-damage clearance. Father does not mind this so much.' Ricardo hesitated. 'From the camp,' he said sadly, 'we could hear Liverpool and Birkenhead being bombed. We heard the noise. We could see the sky. It was red with fire.'

Kezzie thought of the firewatchers like her granddad who would have been on duty. What could they possibly do, confronted with hundreds and hundreds of incendiary bombs setting the trail for the main bombers to follow? What would he do when they started dropping on Clydebank What would they do?

'They will wait now until the winter is over,' said Ricardo 'Then when the weather is better they will return.'

He was proved right. At the beginning of spring 1941 the bombing spread to other locations.

'It seems to be the ports that they are targeting,' said her granddad. 'It's up to our nightfighters. The RAF can keep them out of the skies by day but not in the dark.'

Kezzie's work had increased with the Red Cross to such an extent that most nights she returned home exhausted. Ricardo had to report each day to the police station and there were still some areas where he was not allowed to travel. So he worked mainly in the shop and Kezzie did the deliveries Not that he or Peg minded at all. They took such joy in each other's company. With baby Alec they seemed to make a complete family and Kezzie was happy for them.

Each night as Granddad was leaving to firewatch Kezzie was usually returning from her duties and, as he was out most nights, she slept in his bed. Lucy was growing bigger. She was now nine years old and took up a great deal more room.

One night in March Kezzie came home around eight o'clock. Lucy was already bathed and in bed.

'I warmed the stone pig and put it in the bed for ye,' said her granddad. He hugged her as he left for his firewatching. Every family was the same. Working all hours to keep the troops supplied and their spare time taken up with voluntary work. Her granddad's post was down by the docks.

'Good job I like ships, isn't it?' he had said.

The yards would be the first to get hit if Clydebank is attacked, Kezzie thought, and they would almost certainly come off worst.

She was wrong.

That Thursday night, the thirteenth of March, Kezzie gave her granddad his sandwiches and a bottle of cold tea. She smiled as she watched him pack it in with his gas mask and helmet. She had bought him a vacuum flask, but he rarely used it. It was an old miner's habit. He insisted that the tea, which would be quite cold by the time he drank it, had special reviving powers.

She shut the door behind him and peered into the bedroom. Lucy was asleep. Kezzie took some soup from the pot, then undressed quickly and slipped into the warm bed in the little room off the kitchen.

She was fast asleep with the door closed over when the first alarm sounded.

# 15

# 1941: The Sirens Go Off

The noise of the air-raid siren woke Lucy almost at once She sat up in fright, clutching the rag doll in her hands What was it? A dreadful screaming noise pierced through her head, the wailing going on and on, like an animal being tortured She slipped out from under the blankets, shivering as her bare feet touched the cold linoleum, and trotted quickly through to where Kezzie lay asleep.

'Kezzie,' she whispered, 'Kezzie '

Her sister's eyes were closed fast Dark smudges of exhaustion showed beneath the sockets Lucy shook Kezzie gently.

'Kezzie,' she whispered again

Kezzie didn't stir. Her mouth was partly open and her breathing was regular and deep Lucy waited a moment or two She could still hear the awful sound echoing round the streets, coming right into her house, climbing higher and higher. She held her doll more closely to her and whispered in its ear.

'What is it?' she asked What is it, Kissy?'

Then suddenly Lucy knew what it was It had been weeks, months even since she had heard that particular noise It was the warning The one Granddad had told her about She had laughed, and thought it was a great game when he had made her practise what to do Go into the hall, put on her coat, take her gas mask and run all the way downstairs Right out the back entrance of the close, and she hadn't to stop until she reached the concrete shelter They had races to see who was the fastest She usually won

She puckered her face It was definitely the warning noise, the air-raid siren to let you know that the enemy was coming They would be in the sky now, flying towards them to drop bombs on their head Yet . . . it didn't seem right The noise wasn't the same as before Perhaps it was a trick, a joke, a made up game Lucy shivered again She was quite cold She didn't like this game But now there seemed to be more noise Other sirens were joining in, rising and falling all over the town

So . . . she should wake Kezzie and go downstairs.

Her granddad's voice was in her ear. "If a siren goes you *must* go to the shelter Promise me you *will* go, Lucy. No matter how tired you are, no matter how cosy and warm in your bed Don't snuggle under the blankets Promise me that you will get up at once and hurry outside".

And she had promised Standing solemnly in front of her granddad, she had promised.

But now she couldn't wake Kezzie What should she do?

Lucy took a handful of Kezzie's hair, and tugged gently It didn't seem to bother her She shook her shoulder and called her name Nothing Desperately she grabbed a great chunk of Kezzie's hair and pulled hard Kezzie turned and roughly pushed her sister's hand away. She moaned something in her sleep, then settled down again Lucy closed her own eyes 'Sorry Kezzie,' she said, and yanked the long brown hair even harder.

'Don't,' said Kezzie sharply She moved across and pulled the bedclothes around her

Lucy was now completely at a loss She couldn't wake Kezzie up, and she had tried, really tried. She looked around the little room It was very dark, with no windows, the only light coming through the kitchen from the tiny oil lamp left burning in the hall Perhaps if she closed over the little door and crept in beside Kezzie then the planes in the sky wouldn't see them, and they would be quite safe

Just the same as being in the shelter, she thought. In fact, better, because here it was warmer and not so smelly and damp.

In fact . . . maybe it was only another false alarm Lucy raised her head and listened Faintly in the distance she could hear yet another wail starting, rising and falling like some dreaded banshee.

She touched Kezzie again She didn't stir. She would have to give up *Nothing* was going to wake her sister.

Lucy went out of the small room and into the kitchen She slid quietly between the curtains and the window and edged the blackout board to one side Far away across the roofs she could see lights in the sky Long white pencils of white stretching across the darkness, moving, crossing and recrossing In the distance she saw a strange sight. Big white mushroom shapes floating down, dropping behind the houses and across the river and then suddenly the sky was full of colour. Great sparklers and fireworks, cartwheels and rockets everywhere

It was very exciting Like a party with special fireworks She could hear noises now, thuds and cracks and great bangs, mostly in the distance but coming nearer to her

Lucy watched for a minute or two longer and then turned and slipped back into the room She was cold now Perhaps she should just go back to bed Kezzie was too tired to get up. She worked long hours, first in the café and then in the ambulance, driving And if this noise didn't wake her then *nothing* would

On her way back to bed Lucy passed the kitchen table, where the bowls and spoons and the jug of milk were set out for breakfast in the morning

Kezzie slumbered on, in a deep untroubled sleep She was walking in the park It was sunny and warm, and she was hand in hand with someone, but when she turned her head she couldn't see the person's face. She could hear noises, like children crying, and she knew it should worry her, but she didn't care. She was happy.

Michael Donohoe was in her dream. He shouldn't be there, yet she was not at all surprised to see him. He was standing by the fountain and he was laughing. Smiling and joking the way he always did. And there was a great ache in her heart because she knew he wasn't real. And then he said something to her. But she couldn't hear him. And he called out again, and turned to look at the fountain, at the falling water. And the water was falling, falling from the sky. There was rain on her face, soaking her hair, running down her chin, and she was laughing because she was so wet. But the liquid on her face was not pleasant. She wiped it away in annoyance.

'Don't,' she said in her sleep. Her neck and the top of her dress were soaked. She tried to dry herself. Her hands touched the soft fabric of her nightdress. Kezzie opened her eyes.

'*Lucy!* What are you doing?'

Lucy looked at the empty milk jug in her hands. She took a quick step backwards.

'Kezzie,' she gabbled. 'The sirens are making an awful noise. Granddad said we must get up and go to the shelter if the siren went off. I couldn't get you awake so I . . . I . . .' She looked again at the jug in her hand.

Kezzie lifted her old Gladstone bag which they kept by the front door. Inside it had the family papers and photographs, birth certificates and ration books.

'Wait,' said Lucy. She ran back and picked up her dolly.

They passed Mrs Sweeney's house. She was locking her front door.

'Bother,' she said and turned back.

'What have you forgotten?' called Mary Price from the

next landing.

'The ration books,' said Mrs Sweeney. 'I'll just run back for them.'

Mary Price yawned and leaned against the wall.

'You go on, Kezzie,' she said. 'I'll wait for Mrs Sweeney.'

Kezzie went down to the first floor. The three little boys were lined up outside. Their mum was getting the pram out of the lobby.

'Need a hand?' asked Kezzie.

'No,' she smiled. 'My man's at home tonight. Thanks anyway.'

Kezzie went down to the ground floor. The noise increased as she got lower down, fire bells mixing with sirens and police horns This was no false alarm or ARP practice. She went to the close mouth. The baffle wall was directly opposite the exit. It blocked her view of the street and the sky. It really was *very* noisy, she thought. Now that she was almost outside she could hear the crack and thump more clearly. Kezzie craned her neck forward and looked at the sky. Great fingers of light criss-crossed the skies above her She could hear the ack-ack battery at Duntocher and out in the river a warship was firing away for all it was worth She saw a plane quite clearly, an enemy raider flying low almost directly above her. Grey metal glinting in the beam of the searchlight. It appeared to be trapped in the blinding glare, another locked on to it, and then another, and then, just as suddenly they lost it, and it was gone.

So they have come, thought Kezzie. Her heart began to thud heavily but she felt quite calm as she thought out what to do She looked above her head, at the roof which had been reinforced with thick steel tubing. Should she stay here or make a run for the shelter? Perhaps she should wait for the others? She heard Mrs Sweeney's door bang and the sound of her shrill voice. One of the little boys started crying. Better not to wait, she thought. They would be coming down the stairs in a moment, carrying the wee one with the pram. It would be too crowded here in the close for all of them. Better to go on ahead and set out the blankets for the children.

Kezzie took a firm grip of Lucy's hand in one of her own and, grasping her Gladstone bag in the other, she took one step outside.

At that precise moment, a high-explosive land-mine scored a direct hit on the tenement opposite and blew the whole street to bits.

# 16
# Blitzed!

A great blast of air plucked Kezzie and Lucy off their feet and slammed them both violently against the side wall of the close The rag doll was abruptly snatched from Lucy's grasp and the Gladstone bag from Kezzie's hand Then the whole front of the building sheared off and collapsed into the street, and the remainder tumbled in upon itself

Neither of them made a sound, not a cry nor a whimper All the air in the lungs was torn out of their bodies as the explosion impacted through the close With a shattering roar a huge invisible giant cuffed them both into oblivion

And then the masonry was falling, floor after floor, crashing down and down, crushing the life out of everyone, destroying all in its path Further down the road the gas main fractured Seconds later a spark ignited, and with a loud bang the gas caught fire at the point where the pipe was broken At the far end of the building the gable end of the house still stood The whole structure shuddered and teetered precariously From time to time small pieces of brick and plaster broke off and fell down into what had been the back green

Elsewhere in the town the rescue services were working themselves to a standstill Among the many fires started, the ones at Singer's vast timber yard and Yoker Distillery, which had been set alight almost at once, were the worst The huge quantities of inflammable material in both places meant that it was almost impossible to extinguish them The main bomber groups which followed used the fires as target guidelines One of the biggest water mains, which brought water down from the hills to the town, was destroyed early on by a bomb, and three of the Auxiliary Fire Service Stations were also put out of action at the start of the raid A call went out to neighbouring authorities Sixty-five extra units rushed to help. It wasn't enough The inferno raged on.

Then the parachute mines and the high explosive bombs started falling. Whistling down from skies bringing devastation and death.

By the time the all-clear sounded and dawn came, there was hardly a street in Clydebank without a fatality. Hundreds of civilians had been killed, and hundreds more seriously injured.

It was at first light on the Friday morning that a rescue party reached the place where Kezzie's tenement used to be.

'Gas main gone here,' said the patrol officer He took his notepad and scribbled down some information Then he tore off the sheet and handed it to the young boy who was the messenger for his team. 'Here, son, see if you can get back to HQ and get that one marked up ' He watched as the boy mounted his bike and wobbled off in the direction of the town hall. He grinned at his deputy who was standing beside him. 'Jim's been blown off that bike three times already and he's still determined to ride it.'

'With nearly every telegraph line down, it's just as well lads like him volunteered,' said the deputy. 'We couldnae manage without them.'

The two men surveyed the remains of the tenement block The deputy shook his head 'Don't think anyone got out of that, do you, George?'

George Murdoch shook his head He consulted his notebook 'According to the warden for this area none of them got to the main shelter So . . .' He chewed his lip for a minute 'The only chance ye'd have . . . is if ye were directly under the steel beams at the close mouth '

'Even then ' The deputy shook his head

'Aye, ye're probably right, Willie. But I'll just go and take a wee look.'

'Watch out for that gable end, George. Ah don't like the look of it at all.'

The patrol officer squinted up at the wall. It was as though the end of the tenement had been sliced off with a huge carving knife. Each floor lay exposed to the world. By the fireplace on the first floor was a wooden clothes horse with little vests and pants hung to dry. On a mantelpiece in one room sat two wally dugs with a clock in between. The clock was showing the correct time. On the top floor the table was set for breakfast. The whole structure wobbled precariously.

George Murdoch smiled. 'Aye, Willie,' he said. 'Ah'll keep my eye on it. Ah'm none too happy about it myself.'

He clambered over the ruins and among the wreckage to where he judged the safest part of the building had been. He hunted around and called out loudly for several minutes. He waited for a bit, calling again and again, then, squatting down and putting his ear to the ground, he listened. After a while he began to make his way back. Willie came to meet him.

'Nothing?'

'Nothing.'

'We've got a runner from HQ sayin' they need us two streets away.' The deputy handed him the scrawled message.

Behind them the building groaned and shifted slightly. The two men took a last quick look around.

'There's somethin' there, beside that pipe.' George Murdoch had seen a small object which had been flung aside by the explosion.

'It's only a doll, George,' his deputy said, and kept walking.

'Well, if there's a doll, there might just be a child close by.'

George Murdoch clambered over the pile of bricks which had been the baffle wall, erected to protect any bomb blast going through the close As he bent down to pick up the rag doll he caught sight of a small hand sticking out from under the rubble.

'Hang on a minute!' he called He knelt down and took the child's hand in his own.

It was quite cold.

'Oh, no.' He barely spoke the words It was now seven a m and he had been working since just after the siren had gone at nine the previous evening He was weary, his body tired and his mind stunned with the cases he had dealt with during the night 'Wee kids,' he'd told his wife on the one occasion he had nipped back to his own house to get a cup of tea and collect a spare tin helmet, 'that's the worst to deal with Some burnt beyond recognition Whole families have been wiped out Is this what the world has come to? That we put our children in the front line?'

His big rough hand closed over the frail little one

'Not another wean,' he said aloud He rubbed his eyes with his sleeve 'I don't think I can go much more of this '

'Come out of there, George,' the deputy shouted again That wall's goin' to collapse, and you'll be under it if ye don't move yerself '

'Aye, aye ' He got to his knees And as he did so, his years of first aid training made him instinctively check the wrist before he let go Just before he dropped the child s hand he automatically felt for the pulse

He had turned his face away The sight of the small fingers with the rosy pink nails covered in plaster dust had disturbed him When he thought about it later he reckoned his sense of touch was that bit more alert, his fingertips a fraction more sensitive as they located the point where the child's life blood throbbed through the artery from the heart

'Bloody hell,' he muttered and started to scrabble frantically at the rubble.

'What are ye doin', George?' called one of the team, glancing back.

'A pulse,' he yelled. 'I've got a pulse. This wean's alive!'

'Ye'll need tae stop.' His deputy was beside him now. 'Look,' he pointed at the end wall of the tenement. High above them a large piece of flooring had worked loose and the joist ends were slipping out of the wall plate. 'We'll get some steel rope and drag it down from the other side. Then we free this child.'

'How long d'ye think that'll take?' asked George.

'Half an hour, maybe.'

George looked down at the little hand he still held in his own. 'This wean canny wait half an hour,' he said.

Willie sighed. 'Ah thought ye were going to say that.' He knelt down beside his mate. 'We'll need to do it brick by brick,' he said 'Any big movement and you an' me are goin' have right sair heids the morrow.'

George Murdoch put his hand on his friend's shoulder. 'Ye don't need to wait, Willie,' he said.

'Aye, I do,' said Willie. 'But I'll tell the rest of the squad to stand back.'

Twenty minutes later they brushed the thick grey dust from Lucy's hair and face. She opened her eyes.

'My sister,' she said distinctly. 'My sister was beside me. Will you look for her, please?'

Kezzie was easier to find. Slumped in a sitting position, she was tucked right down into the cavity made by the steel piping which had bent under the force of the explosion to form a protective ring around both her and Lucy. She was unconscious.

The two men didn't like to question the younger child but she was the only person alive and able to speak

'Anyone else, pet?' they asked her as they carried her and

Kezzie towards the stretchers. 'Did any other person come down the stairs. Was there anyone with you at the end of the close?'

Lucy turned her big blue eyes on them both and thought hard. She shook her head. 'They were just about to,' she said, 'Mrs Sweeney and Mary. We heard them talking on the landing above, with my three wee cousins . . .' She stopped. 'But they didn't actually come down. They were still on the stairs. Kezzie said not to wait. That we'd meet them at the shelter. We went to the end of the close to step outside . . .' Her voice faltered. 'I don't remember anything else.'

George Murdoch and his deputy exchanged looks. The tenement staircase had been completely obliterated.

'We'll move on,' said George to his team, 'and send a clearing squad in.'

'Could I have my dolly?' said a small voice

George Murdoch regarded Lucy gravely. The neck and shoulders of the little girl he had just rescued were badly gashed, and he was sure that her wrist was broken. Yet she had not made a murmur as he had worked to free her.

One of the stretcher-bearers tutted in exasperation 'We've got more important things to do than look for a doll.'

'Oh, I don't know,' said George. 'That seemed like a very important dolly to me. Just give us a minute here, mate.' He passed Kezzie on to the next person in the line, then moving very slowly he went back across the rubble and reached down into the hole.

He lifted Lucy's doll and held it up high for her to see

'Got it!' he cried triumphantly.

'George! Watch out! The wall's going!' yelled Willie

The ARP warden tucked the rag doll swiftly into his belt and then raced for his life across the debris He jumped clear just as the gable end of the building crashed behind him

# 17
# Buried Alive

Kezzie felt as if she had toothache in each separate part of her body There was a throbbing pain at the back of her skull, and there seemd to be a weight pressing on her chest. She opened her eyes very slowly. She could remember going to bed last night . . . but after that . . nothing She looked around her She seemed to be in school. There were benches and desks piled up at one end of the drill hall, and when she raised her head she could see that she was lying on the floor along with a long line of other people Suddenly she was aware of the noise Women sobbing, children shouting, babies crying. She gave a moan and lay back down again.

'Kezzie,' said a voice beside her

She turned her head.

'Lucy,' she whispered 'What has happened?'

'We've been blitzed,' said Lucy. 'A bomb dropped right in our street. A big one,' she added

'What time is it?'

'Morning-time They said they'd give us breakfast soon, if we waited '

'Waited?' Kezzie repeated the word stupidly

'Yes,' said Lucy 'After they fixed my wrist and bandaged me up, the lady said we could be sent on somewhere else, or wait until later I said we'd wait here ' She looked at Kezzie 'I made the decision,' she said importantly, 'because you were knocked out I thought we'd best find out about Granddad before we went away '

Kezzie reached over and took Lucy's hand 'You're a very

clever girl,' she said. 'We'll go home now and get some clean clothes and wait for Granddad there.'

'You don't understand, Kezzie,' said Lucy patiently. 'It's all gone Our house, everybody's house. They've been crunched up in the explosions All of them.'

'Everything gone?' asked Kezzie. 'Everything?' She suddenly remembered that she had been carrying the Gladstone bag. 'My bag?'

Lucy nodded.

'We have absolutely nothing left?' Kezzie asked again.

'Just this,' Lucy grinned at her sister. She held up her rag doll.

The next moment Kezzie didn't know whether she was laughing or crying.

As soon as she felt able, Kezzie left the first-aid post and set out for Casella's café. The nurse in charge had told her that, apart from concussion and bruising, she had escaped lightly. She recommended rest for a few hours, but Kezzie knew that her granddad would be wild with worry and the café seemed the most sensible place to go . . . if it was still standing.

She held Lucy close to her as they made their way through the stricken town There were great piles of rubble where there had once been rows of tenements Ruins of homes stood stark in the lightening sky, wedge ends of buildings with their insides ripped out They came across a trolley bus which had its roof torn off. There were dead bodies still sitting on their seats, while some had been flung into the road Huge bomb craters made the roads impassable in places, and many streets had been cordoned off, as the police and rescue teams discovered more and more delayed action bombs The tram rails were twisted out of shape and corkscrewed into the air Pathetic groups of people huddled around mobile canteens which had been set up to distribute cups of tea. Kezzie pulled Lucy in against her coat and tucked her head under her arm They stumbled on.

The little café, wedged in between the tall tenement blocks, had survived. They had just turned the corner into the street when they saw their granddad He ran and gathered both of them in his arms

'I've been back and forwards to Dalmuir a dozen times,' he said, 'checking every church hall and first-aid post in between '

'How are you?' Kezzie asked him.

'One bomb,' he said bitterly. 'One bomb dropped inside the perimeter of the yard. All the rest . . .' He stopped speaking, and looked at Kezzie. 'It's very bad,' he said. 'The town's almost completely gone '

'We know,' said a small voice beside them They both looked down at Lucy. 'We saw it, Granddad,' she said.

He took them quickly into the café and sat them down All the windows had been blown out, but the Biagis had swept up the mess, and hung out a sign saying 'Free Tea and Sandwiches'.

They had spent the night in their Anderson shelter.

'A beautiful shelter,' proclaimed Signora Biagi 'A wonderful shelter. There is none other like it in all of Clydebank '

'Well, perhaps just one,' laughed Ricardo 'I built another for Peg and the baby in her back green, and dug it twice as deep ' He looked anxiously at the café clock. 'I thought she would have arrived by now I think I'll go and see if all is well with them '

'I'll go with you,' said Kezzie, 'and then afterwards I'll go to the first aid post There must be something I can do to help You wait here until one of us comes back,' she told Lucy.

'I can look after myself,' said Lucy primly 'After all,'

she reminded Kezzie, 'it was *me* who got you rescued

The area where Peg lived had been badly damaged Each and every street had been hit. Second Avenue, Radnor Street, Granville Street, all were destroyed Schools and churches had been burned out, the fire station and the pub were completely gutted There was hardly a wall intact anywhere As they progressed further and further, Ricardo became more and more silent Instinctively both of them began to hurry By the time they reached the end of Peg's road they were running They scrambled around the deep crater which marked the beginning of her street and climbed across a huge pile of rubble.

Ricardo clutched Kezzie's arm 'Jesu Maria!' he whispered

He took a few paces forward and then stepped back He looked around hopelessly 'What do we do? What do we do?' he cried.

Kezzie herself was trying to come to terms with what was in front of her There was no part of the building left standing, and the ruins were charred and black It must have taken a direct hit

Kezzie thought Ricardo was about to start running in circles He bent over, doubling up, holding his stomach, as though someone had given him a violent blow He stayed almost on his knees for a moment and then he straightened and began walking up and down, running his fingers through his hair, moaning and crying

'Peg, Peg ' He turned beseeching eyes on Kezzie 'Do you think she is alive? Could they still live, under that?

Kezzie didn't know what to say to him

'Where was the Anderson shelter exactly? she asked

But Ricardo was not listening to her He was striking his head with his hands and sobbing

'Ricardo!' she shouted at him Tell me where the

Anderson shelter should be.'

Suddenly a fierce yelling voice sounded behind them. 'What are you doing here? This area has been cleared.' An ARP warden was running towards them.

'We knew . . . know,' Kezzie corrected herself, 'someone in that building. A young woman and a baby'.

'The building took a direct hit. No one came out of it, nor are they likely to now,' said the warden. 'We searched that area thoroughly.' He looked at the boy in front of him. 'Sorry,' he added. 'Now I'm going to have to ask you to leave. There's an unexploded bomb in the street.'

'No,' wailed Ricardo. He fell to his knees. 'No, no. I beg you.'

The warden spread his hands. 'Look, son, I'm sorry. Truly I am. At the moment there's nothing else anybody can do.'

'Well, there might just be,' said a voice behind them.

Kezzie turned. It was her grandfather.

'I guessed you might need help here,' he said. He turned and surveyed the remains of the tenement. 'This is bad,' he said slowly, 'very bad.' He went over to Ricardo and shook the boy roughly by the shoulder. 'There's work to be done here,' he said. 'If you can pinpoint the exact location of the shelter then we'll try tunnelling in.'

The ARP warden touched his sleeve. 'I can't ask anyone to help you do that. That's above and beyond. You'll need to get volunteers.'

'I only need the one,' said Kezzie's granddad. He nodded at Ricardo. 'An' I think I've got him here already.'

Ricardo dragged his jacket off and handed it to Kezzie. He rolled up his sleeves. 'Now,' he said, 'we dig now.'

'No,' said John Munro, 'we prepare properly first.' He took his pipe from his pocket and sucked on the dry stem for a minute or two as he surveyed the job. 'I need a pick and a shovel and some stout props.' He spoke to Kezzie.

'This will take hours. You'd be better helpin' somewhere else, lass.'

Kezzie knew that part of the reason that he advised her to leave was that he wanted her out of danger She gripped Ricardo's hand.

'Be calm,' she said, 'and hope. My granddad was the best mining engineer in the west of Scotland If they're alive under that then he'll get them out '

# 18
# Evacuation

Kezzie called in at the nearest first aid post, which was operating out of the local primary school, to see if there was anything she could do. The warden noted her name and details.

'We need help with everything,' he said. 'You can make tea, dress wounds, take names and addresses, whatever.' He paused and licked the end of his pencil. 'Anything in particular you're good at?' he enquired.

'I worked as an assistant in a doctor's surgery in Canada,' she said, 'and I've driven an ambulance a few times.'

He thought for a moment. 'Unfortunately,' he said, 'we don't have an ambulance. Though there are folk here who could certainly do with being in hospital.'

Suddenly Kezzie remembered Casella's old van.

'I don't know whether it would be of any use,' she said, 'but . . .'

She thought the man was going to kiss her. Within half an hour Kezzie had returned to the café, told Ricardo's mother and aunt what was happening and checked that Lucy was all right.

'Of course I'm all right,' said Lucy scornfully.

She had on an apron which was several sizes too large for her and was standing in the kitchen making sandwiches. Her face turned pale when Kezzie told her that Peg and Alec were missing, but glancing quickly at Ricardo's mother she said firmly, 'If Granddad's there, then we shouldn't worry.'

When Kezzie returned to the first aid post the warden

had two patients ready for her He handed her some notes 'We've no doctor here, so I've done my best One of them's right poorly I think he needs a blood transfusion We can't give you an attendant, so you'll have to stop at least twice on the way and check his wound's not leaking too badly Take him to the Glasgow Western, and pick up anything you can by way of medical supplies Mind what I say now, *anything* Steal it if you have to,' he called out after her as she set off.

As she drove the long hazardous road to Glasgow, Kezzie was glad that she had something on which to concentrate her mind to stop her thinking of Peg and baby Alec buried under tons of brick and stone The roads out of town were still being cleared and she was diverted many times The van jolted and juddered over ruts and around craters, but eventually she managed to get onto the Boulevard There she was able to pick up speed, and after checking her patients one last time she put her foot down on the accelerator pedal and didn't stop until she reached the hospital.

Casualties had been coming in all night, from Hillhead and Hyndland in the west end of the city Kezzie checked her patients in, managed to beg some supplies, and set out on the return journey to Clydebank

And as she worked on through that day Kezzie knew that she would never forget the sight of the rows of covered bodies lying in lines by the side of the road Those who had not survived, children, babies, rich and poor, wrapped in any available covering, blanket, table cover, curtain and carpet rug Nor would she forget the rescue workers and relatives, as they dug in the rubble, many with their bare hands, their faces grey with dust, grey with fatigue and grey with grief

In the early afternoon while queuing at a mobile canteen she found herself standing with Mr Sweeney and his son

They were part of a team working with the Royal Engineers trying to repair one of the burst water mains. Kezzie knew that Mrs Sweeney's body had been found, and she now lay in the emergency mortuary at the High School in Janetta Street.

'I'm sorry,' said Kezzie.

The son nodded quickly and looked away. Mr Sweeney said, 'She liked you, Kezzie. Not many folk got on with her. She had a sharp tongue,' he sighed, 'but it was just her way. She liked you though.' He studied her more closely. 'You look a bit peaky, hen. Take a rest sometime.' Then he picked up his tea and sandwiches.

It was so inadequate, thought Kezzie, as she watched the two men walk away. 'I'm sorry,' she had said. What good did that do? How did her 'being sorry' help them, or Mary Price, or the three little boys and their parents? Why was she alive and they weren't?

Around half past three, she had parked her ambulance in the school yard and was taking stretchers from it and folding blankets, when the warden came to speak to her.

'There's someone here to see you,' he said. 'Take an hour's break,' he added, 'and that's an order.'

Kezzie walked around the side of her van into unexpected sunlight. Her grandfather was standing there. He had his cap pushed to the back of his head and he looked mighty pleased with himself.

'You found them?' Kezzie hardly dared breathe the words.

He nodded. 'A bit battered about they were, but we got to them. And four others.'

Kezzie leaned against the ambulance door, her senses swimming with relief. 'Are they safe?' she asked. 'The baby . . . how is he?'

'Yelling like a soldier,' said her granddad. 'It was his bawling that made us realise that we were digging in the right direction. It was a difficult one. There were a few times when I thought the whole lot was coming down on us.' He looked down at his hands. 'I never thought I'd be doing anything like that again.'

Kezzie could imagine her granddad working away under the ground. The mining skills gained over half a century proving useful in circumstances no one could have foreseen. His ear sensitive to every sound, every little creak or groan above alerting him to secure a prop, or shore up some more earth before moving on.

'I'd say that, in some cases, it might be a better way of rescuing folk that are trapped. Safer than clearing the rubble from the top, I reckon. Anyway, the chief warden for the area came to take a look, and he wants to see me later.'

Kezzie and her Granddad went to the café. Peg was not well at all. Her clothes were torn and her face and arms were bleeding from a dozen different scratches and cuts. Sitting in the kitchen, dazed and covered in bruises, she was scarcely able to hold a spoon to her mouth.

'We need to get her out of here,' Ricardo whispered to Kezzie. 'But my mother and my aunt won't leave the café now. And, even if they did . . .' He paused, then pointed through the open door to where a weary line of people were waiting for a hot drink and some food. 'I couldn't go away knowing that I'm needed here. I don't know what to do.'

Kezzie touched his arm. 'I think I may know the best solution,' she said.

All day special buses had been taking refugees out of the town to emergency centres in the surrounding areas. Kezzie knew that they had been going to places as far away as central Scotland. Relief had been offered by many towns, including the ones near her own home village, Kirkintilloch and Shawcross.

She took Lucy by the hand and led her outside where

they could speak without interruption. Kezzie sat her sister down beside the Anderson shelter and knelt beside her.

'There are things we need to talk about, Lucy,' she said. 'Serious, important things.'

The blue eyes looked at her steadily.

'Granddad says we will more than likely be bombed again tonight. He is going to remain here because the rescue teams will need help. I think that I also should stay to drive the ambulance.' She paused. 'But we have to get Peg and Alec far away before night-time. Peg isn't well enough to care for the baby by herself. She needs someone with her.' Kezzie met Lucy's gaze and did not look away. 'I want you to go with them,' she said.

Kezzie felt Lucy's hand tighten in her own. She leaned forward and stroked her sister's hair. 'I know that we decided that our family would never be separated, but . . . well, Peg and Alec are just like family. And Ricardo feels he has to keep the café open, so there is no one else.'

Lucy nodded slowly as Kezzie finished speaking. Then she said, 'I might never see you and Granddad again?'

Kezzie knew that she couldn't lie. 'Yes,' she said carefully, 'that is possible. In fact, that's another reason that I'd like you to go. If . . . the worst happens, then at least there would be one Munro left.' She felt her eyes fill up with tears as she spoke.

But strangely, Lucy's face was calm. She thought for a moment or two. 'I suppose that's being sensible.' She gave a huge sigh. 'My teacher keeps telling us that we have to be sensible, especially during a war.' She put her arms around Kezzie's neck and hung on for a moment or two. Just like a little girl again, thought Kezzie. But as they came apart, and she looked at Lucy's face, Kezzie knew that her sister was a child no longer.

There were evacuee buses leaving from various places in

the burgh. After an hour's wait in Dumbarton Road Kezzie managed to get her little group on a bus which was going out to Shawcross.

'Try to get in touch with Aunt Bella,' she instructed Lucy. 'If she can't take you, then she'll find someone who will.' She hugged her sister tightly. 'Be brave,' she whispered. 'No matter how it all turns out, remember I love you.'

'I love you too,' said Lucy.

Kezzie turned away quickly as the bus jerked forward and rattled down the street.

The tiny village of Stonevale had no need to listen to the news broadcasts or read the newspapers that Friday morning. On the Thursday night they saw the glow in the distant sky which told them Clydebank was burning. They had heard the planes, both on the inward and outward journeys.

When word came that homeless families were arriving in the town Bella had walked into Shawcross and spent most of the day in or around the Town Hall. 'If they've managed to survive, then Kezzie will come here,' she told her husband.

It wasn't until early evening that Bella caught sight of Lucy. Still wearing her coat over her nightie and clutching a food parcel, she was dismounting from a ramshackle single-decker bus.

Bella struggled through the crowd in the reception area until she reached Peg and Lucy. She looked around. 'I thought the old man would stay on,' she said, 'but where's Kezzie?'

'She's driving an ambulance, she wouldn't leave,' said Peg.

Bella gave Lucy a big grin. 'So ye came to bide with yer Aunty Bella after all,' she said.

'Kezzie told me it was my duty,' Lucy told her seriously 'And apart from Peg, I'm the only one that baby Alec's really happy with. You know, there's a special way of feeding a baby, Aunt Bella. It's quite difficult, not everybody can do it.'

Bella winked at Peg. 'Well, ah've only had the six myself, hen,' she said, 'but I'll take your word for it.'

Bella looked around the hall until she found the officer dealing with the accommodation arrangements. 'These three are comin' wi' me,' she told her.

Peg grasped Bella's hand as though she would never let it go.

'A big plate o' broth is what you're needin',' said Bella. 'And then a good night's sleep.'

She took them to her own small house and fed them thick soup and potatoes. Then she chased out two of her own children to stay with their cousins, and tucked Lucy and Peg and the baby up in the room bed.

'There now,' she told them, as she turned down the lamp. 'Off to sleep wi' ye. The country air is healing air. I'll see ye and hear all your news in the morning.'

There was still some light in the night sky when the first heavy throb of aeroplane engines sounded overhead. Bella stopped stirring the pot on the fire. She lifted her head and listened. Then she looked at her husband.

'They're no' ours, are they?' she said.

He shook his head.

They both went and stood outside the front door. All along the miners' rows their neighbours were doing the same. And they watched without speaking as the Luftwaffe Third Air Fleet passed high over Stonevale. Formation after formation came across. From Holland initially and then Denmark, from Stavanger in Norway, and air bases in northern France, they flew steadily west towards Glasgow and the Clyde.

In the Clydebank Control Centre the telephone rang. The Civil Defence officer picked it up and listened to the voice on the other end of the line After a few moments he replaced the receiver carefully on its cradle

He turned to face his staff.

'They're coming back,' he said

# 19

# The Sirens Sound Again

The sirens went at 8.40 p.m.

Kezzie's granddad gripped her arm 'Listen, lass,' he said 'There's still time for you to go. No one would blame you.'

She smiled at him 'And what about you?' she asked him. 'Are you going to leave?'

He began to speak. 'I . . .' Then he stopped. 'No,' he said.

Kezzie handed him his tin hat, and picked up her own. 'I honestly think that we don't have a choice,' she said. She pointed round the small hall in which they were sitting. It was situated on the outer edge of the town. Most of the rescue units had been sent out to the relative safety of the perimeter of the burgh to await the calls which would arrive as the raid progressed. 'Many of these people are volunteers who have chosen to remain,' she said. 'And Signoras Casella and Biagi are also staying so that they can open the café tomorrow to help out. We are needed here. You know that. It's a plain fact.'

Kezzie's granddad fiddled with the strap of his helmet. 'This might turn out very bad,' he said.

Kezzie nodded. 'I know,' she said. 'I spoke to Lucy before she left. I think she understands.'

Kezzie watched her granddad. He was ill at ease, buttoning and unbuttoning his tunic, fidgeting with his gas mask. Suddenly he turned to her.

'Kezzie, I would like you to know this, in case anything happens tonight.' He took her hand in his. 'You made my whole world,' he said simply. 'You and Lucy. If you hadn't come back. then I would have had only half a life I want to tell you how much it meant to me.'

Kezzie felt her chin tremble. 'It was the same for us,' she said.

He drew her towards him and put her head on his chest. 'I know that eventually you'll spread your wings. I'm going to tell you this, you mustn't lose sight of your ideals. You've always wanted to be a doctor. so that's what you must do. Don't let anything stop you. Not even this war, no matter how long it lasts.'

He stroked her hair for a moment or two. Kezzie didn't trust herself to speak. Then he gently pushed her away from him, and raised his head. A sudden silence had crept over the little room. Voices hesitated, then spoke in lower tones. Conversations stopped. A steady drone, still some way off, was growing louder by the second. A ragged noise, penetrating the sandbagged walls and reinforced roof, vibrating in the night air. The special Blitzkrieg airborne units were approaching from the east. The Heinkels and Junkers which made up the Luftwaffe bomber squadrons, their engines a throbbing, pulsing underbelly of sound. Now everybody was sitting straight on their benches alert and rigid.

'Let's have a cup of tea,' said the ARP officer loudly.

Kezzie and her granddad took theirs outside. It was a beautiful spring night, the moon pale and luminous in a clear sky. The drumming noise of the aeroplane engines closed around them.

'Those gas mains are blazing away like the fires of hell,' said Kezzie's granddad, 'and there's an oil tank still burning at Old Kilpatrick that they can't get doused. They won't need their pathfinders and incendiaries to mark their way tonight. We're supplying the bloody beacons for them.'

'Look, there,' said Kezzie.

A formation of planes had crossed the river to the south-west. She could see quite clearly the bomb doors opening and the grey IBs with their finned tails begin to fall, dozens and dozens and dozens of them.

'That's the Rolls-Royce works at Hillington they're after,' said her granddad.

All at once the whole world was lit up. Thirty or forty huge searchlights started to sweep the skies, crossing and linking, fusing to form a cone shape. The ground crews swivelling and twisting their beams to hold a great dome of light above the stricken town. Finding the enemy for the gunners to shoot down, deperately trying to dazzle the pilots, keep them to a high altitude, and drive them as quickly as possible away from their target area.

The defence batteries at Duntiglennan roared out, soon joined by the bigger ack-ack guns at Auchentoshan. Shell bursts exploded around and below the aeroplanes. They could hear the thump and crash, the echoes rolling around the Dumbarton hills and out to sea.

The rescue-party foreman came out. 'Message in,' he said. 'There's a warden's post taken a direct hit. Civilians were sheltering in it.'

Kezzie's granddad slipped on his white armband with 'CASUALTY COLLECTION' stitched in black. He spoke to the sergeant. 'I'll be right there.'

He turned to Kezzie. ''Bye, darlin', he said. He looked her full in the face and his eyes met hers. 'Thanks, lass,' he said. And for one brief moment he laid his hand upon her head.

Kezzie remained outside for several minutes after he had gone. The tea turned cold in the mug she held, and she neither heard or saw anything around her.

She started as someone touched her arm. 'They need an ambulance at Parkhall.'

All through the night the people of Clydebank fought to save their burning town. The police and the rescue services, nurses, teachers, student doctors, bus conductresses, messenger boys as young as thirteen years old, veterans of the First World War, struggling desperately to survive and preserve their families and homes.

The beleaguered fire services, with little water, faced a hopeless task as oil tank after oil tank was set ablaze at Dalnottar and Old Kilpatrick, illuminating the targets and making the task easy for each following wave of bombers cruising in and unloading their cargo of death.

An immense and suffocating haze of flame and smoke drifted over the Clyde estuary. The blaze could be seen as far north as Aberdeen and as far east as Edinburgh.

Kezzie was helping with the stretcher cases, which had been laid out at the Janetta Street end of the High School, when a parachute mine dropped at the other end. There was a whistling crack, then a thunderous explosion and the walls on the west side caved in. Kezzie picked herself up and looked around. Plaster and glass were strewn everywhere. One of the messenger boys picked up her helmet and gave her a cheeky grin. He looked at the huge hole in the roof.

'Missed me again,' he shouted up at the sky.

Kezzie's hands shook as she tightened the strap under her chin. Earlier on she had seen a parachute mine which had been caught in a tree during last night's raid. It was a terrifyingly huge black cylinder. At eight feet high, much taller than any man, they measured about three feet across. These and the high-explosive bombs usually followed on after the incendiaries were unloaded. She reckoned the main group of bombers must now be directly overhead. She suddenly thought of Michael. His experience in combat must be similar to this. Under bombardment, comrades falling, wounded and dying beside him, he would fight on. He was doing it, and so must she. This realisation gave her a small measure of comfort. She tightened the helmet strap under her chin. Then she got back into her van and drove off to answer the next call.

Men and equipment had come from John Brown's during the day to cut away the twisted tramway rails and clear roads and streets, but every road was difficult, and some impassable. She was driving along Livingstone Street when an explosion in a building beside her rocked the ambulance and she slewed to a halt. Kezzie noticed the white 'S' for shelter painted on the side of the wall. She climbed down from her cab.

'Need any help?' she shouted.

Two men ran out. One of them looked her up and down. 'Hell, it's a wee lassie,' he called to his mate. 'How old are you, that you're driving that thing?' he asked her.

'Old enough,' snapped Kezzie. 'This is the ninth run I've done tonight. Now do you need assistance or not?'

'You tell him, hen,' his friend laughed out loud.

Kezzie helped an elderly couple and a child who was very badly injured into the back of her van and drove on. The nurse who took the child from her at the first-aid post shook her head quickly, and then placed the little body to one side.

Kezzie turned away. 'Dear God, it must stop soon,' she whispered.

It was nearly dawn when the head warden of her group spoke to her. 'You need a change of clothing, miss.'

Kezzie glanced down at herself. She had spatters of mud and blood everywhere, and one of her sleeves was ripped. Her hands were bruised and scarred where she had helped drag people from rubble. She realised she was still wearing Ricardo's shirt and trousers which she had borrowed earlier.

'Is there somewhere you can get some clean clothes and maybe rest for an hour or two?' he asked.

Kezzie nodded. She would go back to the café. She had driven past it during the night and she knew that it at least had survived. She parked her van and walked the few streets to the Italians' shop. The murky pall of smoke which now hung everywhere was choking and stung her eyes. She practically bumped into Ricardo before she saw him.

'Kezzie, he cried. 'I have been searching for you. Everyone I spoke to said you were with someone else.'

'I know.' She took her helmet off. 'I would be sent one place, and then diverted somewhere else. And I couldn't refuse to take injured people even if I hadn't been called out for them in particular.' She pulled her fingers through her tangled hair. 'Why did you come looking for me?' she asked him.

He didn't reply.

Kezzie looked at Ricardo more closely. He had leaned up against a nearby wall. His eyes were red-rimmed and he had an expression on his face that she had never seen before. Suddenly she knew why. He had been sent to tell her the most terrible news.

'What is it, Ricardo?' she said. 'What is it that you have to tell me?'

'Kezzie.' He drew her close to him. 'Your grandfather has been killed.'

She put her hand across her heart. 'Granddad?' she repeated.

'I'm sorry,' said Ricardo, 'so very sorry. Some people were trapped in the basement of a building. There was an unexploded bomb there. He volunteered to go in.' Ricardo held her tightly. 'It went off. No one could save him.'

'I think he knew,' said Kezzie unsteadily. She frowned. 'Earlier, he tried to tell me how much he cared about us.'

She smiled sadly. 'It was difficult for him. He was so awkward about his feelings.'

'Why don't you cry?' Ricardo said very softly. 'I don't understand you British. Why do you not cry?' He shook his head. 'I don't understand,' he repeated.

And *he* was crying, Kezzie realised. Tears running down his cheeks as he stood helpless in front of her. She reached out her hands to comfort him, and suddenly there were great sobs tearing at her. From inside her heart and soul, a fierce violent grieving took hold of her, and she wept for her granddad. And not only for him, but for her father too, and the mother she had hardly known. For the loss of their company and love. And for all the happy times, the Sunday School trips, the picnics, the outings and birthday parties and Christmases that had happened, and those that now would never happen.

She couldn't stop crying. Her exhaustion after the day's events came rushing in and she was no longer in control.

Ricardo picked her up and carried her to their Anderson shelter. Tucking her up in one of the little wooden-framed bunks, he made her drink some brandy. Then he wiped her face with his handkerchief and knelt down beside her. He held her hand as she lay there and, as Kezzie's breathing eventually deepened into sleep, the resonant note of the all-clear began to sound across the town.

# 20

# Greater Love

'I knew there would be a big turnout to send him off,' said Bella.

She gathered up the teacups and carried them to the sink at the window All day people had called at her house in Stonevale to pay their respects to old John Munro

Many had already spoken to Kezzie that morning, in the kirk and by the graveside Many more had dropped by later to offer condolences.

Kezzie picked up a tea towel and began to dry the dishes. She sighed. 'He had a long life and many friends,' she said. 'But I didn't realise just what a high regard folk had of him.'

'Oh, aye,' said Bella. 'I could have told ye that. Straight, he was. Straight as a die.'

His grave had been covered in flowers. Piled high with great bunches of spring blooms, from ornate bouquets to simple posies, as well as the traditional wreaths. It had been such a stately occasion. The old man brought home to his own town to rest.

A group of former pit workers, ex-miners, white-haired and silent, stood at the cemetery gates, their heads uncovered in the morning sunlight. His workmates from the shipyard, colleagues in the firewatching and rescue services, his cronies from the local welfare club. Colleagues, neighbours, family, friends, all were there. The man's own personal dignity reflected in the burial service.

The rescue-party co-ordinator for the west side, Bob

Black, spent a few minutes telling Kezzie that they were using her granddad's tunnel as an example of safe rescuing procedures.

'We knew there was an UXB in that tenement,' he told Kezzie, 'but he could hear folk calling for help. He volunteered to go in.' He shook Kezzie's hand as they parted. 'He was a brave man.'

She knew that they were having a memorial stone prepared for him, to mark the fact that he had been killed while attempting to rescue his fellow countrymen. It would read: 'Greater love hath no man than this . . .'

Peg had to go back to Clydebank to arrange the funeral of her brother and his wife. Kezzie went with her to help out. The appearance of the town stunned them both. Kezzie had hoped to move back there with Lucy into some type of temporary accommodation. Bella would never say so, but Kezzie knew that her house was overcrowded. She needed the room for her own children. They couldn't expect her to put them up for too long. But now Kezzie saw that it would be many months before any type of property was available in Clydebank. A sign of the relentless pounding the buildings had taken was that, out of the whole town, only eight houses were undamaged by bomb blasts.

To see it in daylight, in the hard glare of the cold spring sunlight made Kezzie feel quite weak. All along the main roads every window was shattered, the chimneys had fallen down, and the streets and pavements were piled with slates, splintered wood, brick and plaster. Raging fires which had now burned out had left the charred and blackened gable ends of tenements poking up into the sky. The housing estates at Radnor and Kilbowie were devastated, the walls of the homes which were still standing, pitted and scarred. Kezzie found it strange that she had managed to function during the actual raid, when hell was pouring out of the skies, yet now she felt confused and disorientated by it all.

It was the desolation, the sight of everyday things from ordinary households lying crushed in the street, which upset her most. A frying pan, a smashed framed photograph, a favourite chair, now broken and useless. Dozens of starving dogs and cats were running wild for days, until an animal clinic was opened in order to have them painlessly destroyed. The sad remnants of little families could be seen searching through collections of furniture and personal possessions left piled in the streets. What was left of them, brothers and sisters with any close relative, tragically small groups of people, trudged to the Rest Centres carrying all they could salvage, sometimes with the youngest member trotting behind, firmly clasping the birdcage.

Peg and Kezzie held on to each other as they made their way through the streets. Clean water for drinking had been brought in barrels from Glasgow and there were long queues holding kettles, teapots or jugs. The YMCA tea cars had parked their mobile canteens outside the church halls. In Casella's café a constant stream of refugees came through the door, where Ricardo, his mother and aunt handed out hot soup and slices of bread and margarine. Each night many people slept on makeshift beds on their floor. They seemed incapable of turning anyone away.

She knew that they also had no space for her and Lucy. Signor Biagi's latest tribunal hearing had agreed that, in the special circumstances, he would be allowed to return to Clydebank. When things settled down, they wouldn't need Kezzie's assistance in the shop. Peg and the baby were now living there. With Ricardo, the three of them made such a compact and joyful unit among the surrounding chaos. Kezzie was deeply moved by their happiness. Each moment was now valued, each measure of time spent together precious.

Kezzie's heart ached for Michael. His company at this time would have lifted her spirits so much. Where was he now? she wondered. Under what foreign sky did he rise in the morning or lie down to sleep at night? Stationed in some far-away place in the hot desert, he would receive in time the letter she had sent giving him her dreadful news Why wasn't he here, so that she could tell him properly, and then he could comfort her? She was so tired that she felt like weeping for ever and never ceasing.

It wasn't openly discussed, but everyone thought that they would be attacked again, some time in the near future, especially as the yards had got off so lightly. Only hours after the all-clear had sounded, an enemy reconnaissance plane had come in at high altitude to assess the damage. Kezzie supposed that it was due partly to her country's spirit and determination that folk were trying to keep production going. In the week following the blitz thousands of workers walked miles from their billets and Rest Centres to return to work. John Brown's, the Royal Ordnance Factory, Singer's, Beardmore's, all struggled to get their output back up. And they were succeeding, they were producing the parts and supplying the forces.

Things were getting back to normal. So . . . she shouldn't feel so bad about thinking of leaving. It was the best thing to do, for both Lucy and herself. She knew that she would have to give up her studies for the present, but she needed time to recuperate anyway, and then to plan for the future. There was some small income due to them from her grandfather's dependency fund, but she would soon have to make better provision for Lucy and herself. Kezzie took out the letter which she had received yesterday and read it again.

*Dear Kezzie,*

*I am sending this via the post office in Shawcross as I know it is the nearest town to your home village. I hope that it reaches you and that you and your family are in good health. It is very difficult to obtain clear news of what Clydebank has suffered in the recent blitz. Due to censorship the newspapers are frustratingly vague, but I have gleaned enough information to realise that you may need some support. Please do come and stay with me, Kezzie, I would welcome an opportunity to repay the debt I owe you.*

*With warmest wishes,*

*Mary Elizabeth Fitzwilliam*

*PS Travel arrangements may be complicated so I enclose the name and address of a friend in Edinburgh. I shall wire him to be ready to secure train tickets for you if need be.*

Kezzie came to a decision. Tomorrow she would take a bus to Edinburgh and find Lady Fitzwilliam's friend. Then she and Lucy would make the journey to England.

# 21

# Travelling South

The train journey from Edinburgh south to England was long and tedious Kezzie was glad that she had managed to beg some books and comics for Lucy, so that she had something to read as they sat squashed together in the corner of one of the crowded compartments They were lucky to have obtained a seat at all At any moment Kezzie expected her sister to start to complain, and she was trying to think of some bright conversation and word games to divert her as soon as the inevitable boredom and petulance began There was little room and the air soon became hot and stuffy, but Lucy said nothing. As the hours passed she squirmed around in her seat a little but still spoke no word of protest.

Kezzie thought about this. Something had altered in her sister since the blitz, some subtle change which she could not quite describe. She recalled when they had been making their farewells to Ricardo and his family, Lucy had been very composed, more so, in fact, than Kezzie Saying goodbye to Peg had been particularly traumatic. The two friends had become so much closer over the past eighteen months. Lucy had suprised them both by suddenly thrusting her rag doll into Peg's hand.

'I want you to keep her,' she said.

'Oh no!' said Peg, giving Lucy her doll back at once. 'I know how much she means to you. You can't possibly give her away.'

'Yes, I can,' said Lucy firmly. 'I don't need her any more.'

Peg looked at Kezzie. 'What do I do?' Peg mouthed the words silently across the top of Lucy's head.

Kezzie shook her own head. She bent down and she spoke to her sister. 'Are you sure about this, Lucy?' she asked. 'Kissy has been with us a long time.'

'Yes,' said Lucy. 'I'm grown-up now, and Alec will need something to cuddle if the bombers come back.' She tucked her rag doll under the little boy's arm.

This was an older and wiser child who now sat beside Kezzie on another part of their travels. And although Kezzie knew that Lucy at some stage must leave her babyhood, she could not help a faint feeling of wistfulness for the little girl who had depended on her for so long.

The quiet countryside passed by on the other side of the glass. First the Lammermuir hills in the distance, a purply gold mantle which encircled the coastal towns and then suddenly the train was running alongside the North Sea itself. Close by the beaches of Gullane and after Dunbar, the water was gentle, and the waves broke in long rolling lines among the sandy dunes. Further out the haar hung cold and damp, shrouding the lighthouses and marker buoys. Beyond them in the deep seas the U-boat wolf packs hunted the British merchant ships in an attempt to starve the island into submission.

Kezzie gazed out of the window. She was almost happy to be away. She needed to distance herself from the devastation and destruction which she had witnessed. She had to have some rest, her mind and body were close to exhaustion. She was weary of this war, of the sacrifices and the constant doing without. The senseless loss of life she had witnessed confused and bewildered her, and the death of her beloved grandfather had brought her down completely. Even the manner of his death, which should have been a source of pride, did not ease her grief. Her emotions were swamped and she felt unable to cope with any of the ordinary things of life. It was in fact Lucy who had organised most of their arrangements. It was she who had comforted Kezzie, had taken charge of her and made her eat when she was too listless to do so. And of them all, only her Aunt Bella had understood her desire to leave Scotland and her friends.

'You go to England, hen. Let this lady friend of yours look after you. You're not running away. If you don't get a rest soon then ye'll have a breakdown, and be no use to anyone.'

The train crossed the border into Berwick-on-Tweed and headed further south. It was hard at times to know exactly where they were as the signposts had either been removed or painted out. They were frequently shunted backwards and forwards, or kept waiting in stations.

In a siding where they had been left for nearly half an hour Kezzie watched a gang of workmen laying some rail track a few yards distant. They had their caps pulled down over their faces as they worked. She put her head on one side. Their manner and appearance was strange, but she didn't know why. Was it the way their trouser legs were tucked into their boots, or how they held the heavy crowbars and pickaxes. What was it that was unfamiliar? One had shirt sleeves rolled up past the elbows, and it was the sight of those slim and pale arms that made Kezzie realise what was different. They were all female. Not such an unusual sight, now, in wartime, she thought, but worthy of comment all the same.

The whole aspect of woman's life and dress was changing. Most of the trams and buses had female conductresses, and many of the older girls in the streets were in uniform. Women were now much less formally dressed in daytime. Headscarves were more usual, rather than a smart hat. Many women pinned their hair up and went hatless. A few were even wearing trousers in public. Kezzie smiled as she remembered her Aunt Bella telling her of one of her neighbours who had started to wear dungarees. This of course had caused great comment in the tiny village of Stonevale, as Bella related to Kezzie.

'Well,' the poor woman said defensively to Bella. 'They're very practical. And I'll be better off wearing them if I have to go into one of these air-raid shelters. You try crawling into an Anderson shelter with your skirt and suspenders on. At least *I* won't be showing off all of next week's washing for everyone to see.'

'Aw, hen,' replied Bella, 'if we do get attacked, an' Jerry starts droppin' bombs, ah'll tell ye one thing. See when we're all running' tae the shelters, they'll be naebody lookin' at your knickers.'

The rest of the passengers on the train also began to realise that the work squad outside was a group of women. There were very many young men on the train: soldiers, sailors and airmen travelling to join their units. Very soon the whistling and catcalls started. The windows went up, carriage by carriage, and further down the train a door opened. Some soldiers jumped out and walked along the track to offer cigarettes. The girls chatted and joked with the young men before the guard eventually blew his whistle and waved them back aboard.

Kezzie studied all the uniforms as they passed. She always felt that little bit closer to Michael if she saw the Argyll and Sutherland tartan or cap badge.

They changed at York to a branch line which skirted Sheffield, ran through Chesterfield and on down in the direction of Derby. The main station was very busy and they had to wait some time for their connection, so it was late evening when the train finally arrived, wheezing and puffing, into the tiny station of West Fenton. Kezzie and

Lucy stepped down onto the platform. They looked around them at the little white-painted picket fencing and the brave display of snowdrops and crocuses in one window-box beside the ticket office. Kezzie smiled. The other had carrots growing in it. There was no indication at all of where they were. It was fortunate that both the guard and the conductor had looked after them so well, and made sure that they knew when to get off. Kezzie gazed at the fields stretching far into the distance on all sides. She picked up the little cardboard suitcase which held all their belongings.

'There must be a post office nearby,' she told Lucy. 'We'll ring Close Manor House from there.'

She took the letter from Lady Fitzwilliam which had the telephone number written on it, and went to speak to the man in the ticket office. He glared at her when she asked for directions to the village.

'Arr,' he said with a thick country burr. 'I don't understand a word of what you've said.' He came out from the little office and peered at Kezzie suspiciously. 'Are you a German spy?' he demanded.

Lucy giggled. 'No,' she said. 'Are you?'

The man narrowed his eyes and looked at her more closely. 'That's a very strange accent you have,' he declared. 'Very strange indeed.'

'Mr Penrose,' a voice called out loudly from behind them. 'This young lady is a friend of mine. Who *do* you think she is? Mata Hari?'

'Most peculiar way of talking,' muttered the man, as he reluctantly returned to his desk.

'My dear, I am so glad to see you once more,' Lady Fitzwilliam took Kezzie's hand and shook it formally. 'And this must be Lucy.'

As Lady Fitzwilliam bent down to say hello, Lucy, with a most natural gesture, kissed her.

Lady Fitzwilliam flushed with pleasure She straightened up and touched her cheek with a gloved hand 'Such a charming child I don't wonder that you travelled so far to find her again.'

She led them outside to where a pony and trap stood in the country road. 'Here we are, my dear I've managed to arrange transport for us Unfortunately we must conserve petrol, so this will have to do You don't mind, do you?' she asked.

Kezzie laughed 'Not at all,' she said. 'I expected to walk.'

There was an elderly uniformed chauffeur standing respectfully beside the pony He was holding its reins and regarding it nervously.

Lady Fitzwilliam introduced them 'This is Samuel,' she said. 'He was my husband's driver Now he is coping very well with this form of transport, aren't you?' she asked him

'A bit more unpredictable than motor cars, ma'am,' he said.

'Nonsense,' said Lady Fitzwilliam firmly. 'I remember distinctly when my husband bought the first Daimler. You were very reluctant to try it out.'

'That was twenty years ago, ma'am,' murmured Samuel 'I've got used to mechanical engines '

'I don't think you should be so worried about driving a horse, even after a gap of twenty years, surely?'

Samuel eyed the pony again. 'It's not so much me being worried about the horse, ma'am,' he said. 'I think it's more a case of the horse being worried about me.'

Lucy had been hopping about, pulling grass from the banks of grass at the sides of the road and trying to feed the animal.

'Can I sit up at the front?' she begged.

Kezzie frowned at her, frightened that Lucy's natural

exuberance would be taken for rudeness

Lucy saw her sister's face 'Please,' she added quickly

Lady Fitzwilliam leaned over and pinched Lucy's cheek with her gloved fingers 'You,' my darling, can do exactly as you wish.'

# 22
# Close Manor

They made their way through the small village of West Fenton, over the level crossing, past some thatched cottages and out into the country. It was like no other part of the world, thought Kezzie.

'It's so . . ' she searched for the word . . . 'so picturesque.'

The evening sky was slatted with long low clouds, lit from behind with the rays of the sunset. The pleasant sound of birdsong, the steady trot of the horse and the wheels turning were all that could be heard.

Kezzie leaned back in her seat, and let the serenity of the English countryside surround her. 'It's quite beautiful,' she said.

Tucked away in an undisturbed part of a traditional British landscape, it appeared to her that nothing had altered here for many years. And I hope it never will, she thought, as they rode along past high hedgerows, fields and meadows.

She knew that the idyll before her was part illusion, of course. Not many miles distant lay Derby, where there was a concentration of heavy and light industry. The Rolls-Royce works were working on the new Merlin engine and turned out the parts for Spitfires and Hurricanes. The town, despite its civilian population, had been a target for the Luftwaffe already, and would continue to be.

But for the moment she could pretend. She and Lucy could relax in this lush and fertile landscape. She did need some rest, some time to recuperate.

They entered a long drive through ornate stone pillars, gravel spitting out from under the horse's hooves as they made their way past the gatehouse.

'This is where I live.' Lady Fitzwilliam pointed to the red-brick building at the top of the drive. There were banks of thick rhododendrons, monkey-puzzles, tall gum-trees, bushy yews and close-clipped box hedges. Croquet hoops were set out on the front lawn, with the mallets and balls lying carelessly to one side. Like a scene from *Alice in Wonderland*, thought Kezzie. She gripped the handle of her bag tightly. How were she and Lucy ever going to cope with all of this?

The horse clip-clopped its way sedately around the manor house to the stable yard at the side, where Samuel helped them dismount. Then, eyeing the animal suspiciously, he led it under cover to unharness it. Lady Fitzwilliam took them through the conservatory and into the house, pulling off hat, scarf, gloves and coat, and discarding them as she went. She waved a hand as Kezzie attempted to collect some of her clothes on the way.

'Samuel will see to them,' she said. 'He knows that I am far too busy to bother with things like that.'

Lucy and Kezzie exchanged glances. Lucy stuck her finger under her nose and pushed it up and to one side, wildly out of shape. Kezzie glared at her sister, but could not help but smile. Lady Fitzwilliam still had all the regal manners that Kezzie could vividly recall from her meeting with her on the boat to Canada.

'Tea,' declared Lady Fitzwilliam, 'we must have some tea.'

She led them into a large kitchen. 'It's Sally's night off,' she tutted in exasperation as she searched in cupboards and looked on shelves for the tea things. 'So inconvenient. I asked her to change, as you were arriving today, but she has an appointment with a young man, so she refused.'

Kezzie could tell that Lady Fitzwilliam considered Sally had seriously neglected her duty by taking the day off which was due to her.

'She did say thát she would lay out some supper,' said Lady Fitzwilliam, looking around her vaguely.

Behind them Samuel coughed discreetly. 'Perhaps if you would care to go into the drawing-room,' he suggested. 'I've lit the fire there, and I will bring through a tray.'

Lucy peered all around her as they followed Lady Fitzwilliam. The large paintings and ornate mirrors which hung on the walls were quite overpowering. The drawing-room where they had tea appeared immense to them. Bella's whole house could have fitted easily into this one room.

'I suppose it is wartime, and one has to make do.' Lady Firzwilliam sighed deeply as she handed Kezzie a plate of sandwiches. 'Everyone has the same story. The young girls now won't come into domestic service. They all run off and join the munitions factory. I don't know why.'

'I expect it's because they are paid so much more,' said Kezzie. 'Also it might be more interesting to have lots of company your own age.'

'I have given these young women employment and their mothers before them,' protested Lady Fitzwilliam. 'They know that I will look after them.'

Kezzie thought about the girls she had seen earlier laying the railway track. 'Perhaps they don't want to be "looked after",' she said. 'Maybe they want to do things for themselves . . . as equals,' she added.

'Equals?' said Lady Fitzwilliam.

'Yes,' said Kezzie. 'Equality of the sexes, for one example. It might actually happen after this war is over. We have made a start, at any rate.'

'Do you really think that this is progress?' asked Lady Fitzwilliam.

'I think that anything that makes people closer to each other is an improvement,' said Kezzie. 'And the war has done that. Men and women are working together, more truly equal than ever before. This is the beginning. And we're not going to let it go.'

'Well,' said Lady Fitzwilliam, as she bit daintily into a sandwich. 'There are things which I don't consider to be quite seemly. Modern manners are extremely . . . casual. And,' she hesitated before she spoke again, 'perhaps we aren't *meant* to be equal.'

'I'm sorry,' Kezzie apologised. She had hardly arrived in this lady's house and it looked now as though she was abusing her hospitality. 'I hope that what I've said hasn't upset you. It's just that we have to work this out. Equality must come. Men and women, rich and poor . . .'

Kezzie thought of the shrivelled and sometimes unrecognisable remains of humanity which she had ferried in her van to the mortuary in the latter stages of the clearing-up operation in Clydebank. The mass burial on the Monday morning for the unclaimed victims, each person wrapped in a simple white sheet. She bent her head into her hands.

'We are all the same in death,' she whispered.

Lucy got up quickly and came and stood beside her. She took Kezzie firmly by the hand.

'My sister is tired,' she told Lady Fitzwilliam. 'She needs to rest.'

'Yes, yes, of course.' Lady Fitzwilliam rose and led them upstairs to the bedrooms she had set aside for them.

As Lucy helped her undress and slide between the sheets Kezzie began to worry about their position in this house. Perhaps she shouldn't have been so outspoken. She could sense that she had disturbed Lady Fitzwilliam and now she was not at all sure that she and Lucy should stay on. In the great feather bed she slipped into sleep and dreamed she was walking in bright green meadows where buttercups and daisies were growing. Yet each time she tried to pick a bunch the flowers withered as she touched them.

In the morning Lady Fitzwilliam brought her some tea.

'Lucy and I have had breakfast and I've sent her to play for a little while,' she said. 'It will give us a chance to talk. Kezzie, I look at your face and I see a young woman who is on the verge of complete exhaustion. Please allow me to take care of you. You must go for long walks, read and eat, and pass some time away from unpleasant things. So, perhaps we should agree not to discuss serious matters such as we did yesterday evening.' She smiled at Kezzie. 'You must understand it is very difficult for an old lady like me, who was born in the last century, to come to terms with all these new ideas. When I was your age I had a personal maid who laid out my clothes, ran my bath and dressed me in the mornings. Yet I read in the newspaper that the Princess Elizabeth has trained as a motor mechanic so that she can service her own jeep, and the Queen herself has a ration book. So I too must change my ways.'

Kezzie and Lucy found that it took them some time to adjust to the house itself. The rooms were huge, the furniture grand and imposing.

'It's staring at me,' Lucy told Kezzie one night, pointing at the wardrobe in her bedroom.

Kezzie laughed, but she could understand her sister's apprehension. The elaborate carvings and curved handles on the triple doors gave the appearance of some strange giant from folklore lurking in the corner. The few clothes which Lucy had been allocated by the relief agencies or given by friends were lost in its depth.

But the very size of the grounds around the manor house were a benefit to Kezzie. She could wander there all day, stroll along the shady paths or walk in the walled garden at sunrise and never encounter anyone. She would choose an isolated spot under a tree to sit with her book or some knitting in the afternoon, and generally fall asleep. Very slowly her mind began to heal, and her dreams at night were less troubled. Lady Fitzwilliam didn't mind Kezzie's need to be on her own. She loved Lucy's company. They spent their time planting vegetables in the kitchen garden, or going for little drives to meet friends in the surrounding villages.

The lilac was blooming, when they heard that Clydeside had been bombed on two more occasions. Samuel was away, so Lady Fitzwilliam herself drove into the nearest town to obtain news.

'Not nearly so severe,' she called as Kezzie came running to meet her on her return. 'Very little damage.'

Still Kezzie fretted, and she hurried to the post office each day until word arrived from Peg confirming this. Peg's letters were full of bright cheerful chatter about Ricardo and the baby. Alec was learning Italian words as fast as English.

*He can say 'I want sweets' in two languages*, Peg wrote, *and he is completely spoiled by everyone. His attempts to eat spaghetti are hilarious.*

'I worry about them,' said Kezzie as she read the latest letter at breakfast one morning.

'She would be very welcome here,' said Lady Fitzwilliam. 'Both she and the baby could have a holiday in the country.'

'She wouldn't leave Ricardo,' said Kezzie. She thought about it for a moment. About the whole situation. Herself and Lucy, the evacuated children and people risking death to stay together. 'And I'm not sure that she should,' she said eventually.

'No, indeed,' said Lady Fitzwilliam When I had the evacuee children billeted here, this village was so remote no parent was able to visit The two that I did have went home after a few months I tried very hard but they were desperately homesick May I ask why you did not send Lucy away? You must have thought she could be safer

'I found it impossible after what had happened to her before, said Kezzie 'Then after Coventry was destroyed we tried to, and she ran away So finally the decision wasn't mine ' Kezzie looked at Lady Fitzwilliam 'Do you think it was so awful not to have made her go? Perhaps I should have insisted She could have very easily been killed '

Lady Fitzwilliam leaned over and grasped Kezie's hand 'I don't blame you,' she said 'I wouldn't have done it ' She wiped her mouth carefully with her cloth napkin, and then, folding it meticulously, she placed it alongside her plate 'Very selfish of me, my dear, I suppose ' She smiled at Kezzie 'However, one can only do as one sees fit at the time History and,' she smiled wryly, 'and one's children will eventually be the judge ' She sighed 'Let us hope that they will not be too harsh As you say, with Peg and Ricardo, their love will survive '

Yes, thought Kezzie, better to be together Michael was now in Egypt and had seen action The news was uncertain and patchy, his letters heavily censored Was he thinking of her as she did of him? How she longed for him, to hear his voice and see his face again, if even only for a short time

The blitzes of May continued City after city was bombed relentlessly, the ports in particular were targeted Liverpool, Belfast, Hull, Clydebank, Plymouth, Portsmouth And then on the 11th of May London suffered the most appalling raid Over a thousand people were killed in one night, bringing London's total of civilian blitz casualties to twenty thousand When the radio broadcast the sombre news, there was a grim and desperate tone to the bulletins. It was several days before they obtained newspapers which gave an account of the damage. The square tower of Westminster Abbey had fallen in, the chamber of the House of Commons had been reduced to rubble. The faces of the rescue workers and the survivors were stunned and bewildered. It seemed as if the famous spirit of the Londoners might be cracking. There were people weeping in the streets.

Lady Fitzwilliam read her newspaper and then she laid it to one side. Her face was white and her hands were shaking. She turned to Kezzie and whispered, 'We can't bear this much longer.'

# 23
# School Lessons

That afternoon Kezzie and Lady Fitzwilliam took a long walk in the country. There was blossom on the trees and the smell of summer days to come and, as they strolled along the lanes, the idea of war and the reality of the blitz seemed many miles away Kezzie breathed deeply and tried to let the warmth in the sweet air act as a balm to her frayed nerves But both of their minds carried the pictures of shattered cities all over Britain which were being relentlessly ground down into dust Suddenly Lady Fitzwilliam stopped at a wooden gate She turned to Kezzie.

'The reports say that the RAF fighter planes shot down twenty-nine of theirs ' Her eyes were tortured and she shredded her gloves with her fingers 'Just twenty-nine destroyed out of over five hundred It's not enough Our boys cannot keep fighting night and day There are too many of them, and too few of us.'

Kezzie put her hand on Lady Fitzwilliam's arm She knew that William being in constant danger was causing his mother unceasing distress She tried to find words to say which might comfort her

'Last year, after Dunkirk,' she said, we were days away from invasion It was the flyers who fought them off Day by day, keeping the Luftwaffe out of the skies It will be the same this time This is a last act of desperation to bring us down It won't work We won't let it '

Lady Fitzwilliam leaned wearily on the gatepost 'William says government intelligence sometimes exaggerate their scores to keep morale up And that the press don't print all of our casualties It is not always the whole truth that we read in the newspapers '

'I know this,' said Kezzie She remembered in the aftermath of Clydebank, the rescue workers and survivors, relatives of the victims, had been extremely upset at government statements which had minimised the damage and the number of people who had lost their lives It had caused great resentment in the town which had suffered so much

What a terrible responsibility the war leaders had Making decisions which involved life or death for thousands of people Trying to keep civilian hopes high and the spirits of the troops to fight on What was the famous quote. *the first casualty of war is truth*'.

She was aware that Lady Fitzwilliam was still gazing at her, as though in some way Kezzie might bring succour and inspiration Kezzie searched in her mind for something to say It was this lady after all who had taken her in, offered her a home when she had none She must try to help her now when she was so desperately seeking reassurance Kezzie hesitated Her next words might not be welcome, but she felt now she had to speak plainly

'I think,' said Kezzie carefully, 'that we should involve ourselves more In the war effort, I mean '

'My dear girl,' protested Lady Fitzwilliam What I do already completely exhausts me What more is there?'

'Yes,' said Kezzie slowly You do at times have rather a hectic round of engagements '

There was the 'Save for a Spitfire' committee, the vicar s wife's weekly knitting bee, and various fêtes, fund raising events and social teas Kezzie knew that Lady Fitzwilliam was actively involved in all of them, and she herself had taken to going along to help out But there was a nagging thought in Kezzie's head that all of this didn't take much effort They were on the fringes of the real war. Others were working harder, doing more Perhaps driving her makeshift ambulance, and being involved in rescuing people first-hand, would make anything else seem tame But now that she felt better in herself, she was more able to contribute, and she knew that she wasn't doing it. Her senses had recovered enough for her to be slightly restless at her own inactivity.

'I know that you don't have evacuated children living here any more,' she said, 'but there are a few in houses round about. The village school has closed. Now, if you count the remainder of the local children, then there are quite a few young people, Lucy included, who are receiving no education.'

'What do you suggest?' asked Lady Fitzwilliam.

'We could have lessons in the house in the morning Samuel could use the trap to collect and return the children to the surrounding farms and houses It would be good for them, and us,' Kezzie added 'I think we need something more positive to do.'

'Yes, my dear. You are, as usual, quite correct. I'm sick to death of sitting around with the same old faces knitting comforters for soldiers ' Lady Fitzwilliam laughed 'And I suppose I must find something more useful to do than embroider a cover for my ration book '

They held the classes in the large dining room At first it was complete chaos They had to beg or borrow exercise books and pencils, and organising the children was extremely difficult Some were overawed by being in the big house, others thought it a wonderful opportunity to run wild Kezzie thought Lady Fitzwilliam was showing great patience in dealing with the more boisterous of them, and told her so

'Well, they are the future, aren't they?' she told Kezzie 'And it is, after all, their fathers who are fighting and being killed on our behalf

It was finally Samuel who found the best way of controlling them and keeping discipline Those who behaved were allowed to drive the horse on the round trip home, those who didn't were sent for an hour in the morning to collect the manure and spread it on the vegetable plots Soon some of the mothers had established a volunteer rota and the lessons and a small play group were held each forenoon

Meanwhile the war, and the restrictions, continued

'Clothing coupons!' Lady Fitzwilliam announced one morning 'Really it is too much Clothing coupons! Whatever next?'

She was reading from the newspaper in tones of great indignation 'And we are to be allowed to utilise our margarine coupons while we await these new vouchers to be printed What a choice to be faced with Dry bread or a new skirt'

Kezzie giggled She imagined Lady Fitzwilliam calling at her hat shop in Nottingham to select something for autumn and being handed a quarter of a pound of Bluebell margarine

Then the rationing of coal was announced The weather was warm and the windows stood open for most of the day but Lady Fitzwilliam was concerned She spoke to Kezzie 'The house is very cold in the winter We are exposed here, sitting as it does on the top of the hill My husband's father planted many of the trees to serve as windbreaks, but the gales come sweeping across at the end of the year The children will be cold,' She frowned If we are short of coal and there is no heating we might have to stop our school lessons'

They began to stockpile wood in the stables Dragging in broken and fallen branches from the trees around the house During the holidays the children helped by making up bundle after bundle of twigs for kindling One of their parents, a local farmer, offered to cut up logs for them

'The only problem is transporting them,' he told Kezzie. 'I'm so short of manpower, half my machinery is lying idle'

'I have driven,' said Kezzie. 'Is a tractor very difficult to learn?'

It was more unstable, she soon discovered, as she hung on to the wheel as it bounced along the rutted tracks They worked hard during the summer, attaching chains to the tree trunks and dragging them back from the woods The farmer was impressed with how she coped with it all He spoke to her one day.

'I'll need help when the harvest comes,' he said 'I don't have nearly enough land girls working Would you come over in the autumn and lend a hand?'

Kezzie didn't dare tell Lady Fitzwilliam, but she practically promised him her help She thought she might enjoy it. There would be company of her own age which she found she missed, and it would make her feel that she was doing something to help the war effort Lady Fitzwilliam would be quite capable of managing their little school with some help from the older children and mothers Whether she would agree with that was another matter She and Kezzie had found that they got on very well together They had even managed to talk politics without disagreeing too violently

Then, in an attempt to restore a mood of resistance and determination, the Government launched a new campaign, 'V for Victory' It was to become a symbol of hope for those in occupied Europe where the BBC broadcast every night There were soon posters everywhere with the distinctive V sign surmounting the flag

One late summer's evening when it was still warm enough to sit outside, they set out chairs in the garden, just below the terrace which ran the length of the back of the house It was quiet and pleasant, and yes . . . peaceful, Kezzie decided. She fetched a cardigan for Lady Fitzwilliam from her bedroom and settled down to read. She could hear in the distance the cries of Lucy and some friends as they played in the long paddock on the other side of the house.

Kezzie was absorbed in her book, so that at first she did not notice the uniformed figure which stepped through the open french windows and walked quietly down the curved steps Long shadows were grouping among the trees at the end of the path Lady Fitzwilliam had fallen lightly asleep Her lips apart, she was snoring gently. Kezzie carefully retrieved the journal which was slipping from her fingers. As she did so she glanced up, and saw the tall young man dressed in the blue of the RAF walking across the lawn towards them Something about the way his left leg slurred as he approached caught her attention. She straightened her head and looked more closely.

'William?' she said quietly.

# 24
# William

Lady Fitzwilliam screamed in delight and scrambled very inelegantly to her feet.

'Darling boy!' she exclaimed. 'You should have warned us. I would have prepared properly for your return,' She smoothed out the skirt of her frock. 'I feel so shabby with this ancient woollen dress. It's several seasons behind in style.'

Kezzie was suddenly very much aware of her own short-sleeved blouse, with its decorated collar and capped sleeves, which was rather worn and very much out of date. William, however, wasn't concerned with any fashion garment whether modern or not. He hugged his mother and kissed her several times and then turned his attention on Kezzie. He gazed at her for several moments then finally spoke.

'Kezzie,' he said. 'You look more handsome than ever.'

She smiled up at him. The thin sandy moustache which she remembered, was now quite a respectable size and his face had matured into a strong firm profile. In his dark blue uniform, with the peaked hat and braid, he looked very attractive.

She grinned at him. 'So do you,' she said

He gave a whoop of delight, and grabbing her round the waist, he spun her about the lawn.

'Behave yourself, child,' his mother laughed and smacked him with her magazine.

'I've got two days,' he declared, 'and the use of a jeep and some petrol. We're not going to waste a second of it'

Lucy was at first terribly shy with William. He had no brothers or sisters and was unused to children, and he treated her with a formality which she could not understand To complicate matters there were the two accents. His, a long slow drawl with many expressions which she found strange and incomprehensible For his part, he was baffled by the speed at which she spoke and the variety of words she used which he had never heard before. He tried hard to be friends but they were awkward in each other's company After dinner they played very politely with a jigsaw on the floor of the sitting room for nearly an hour until he suddenly sat up and snapped his fingers.

'Have you been through the attics yet?' he asked her

When Lucy shook her head he pulled her to her feet

'Oh, jolly good!' he cried 'That means I can be the first to help you explore. I know! We'll find the hamper with the clothes for dressing up Then we can have some super fun tonight.'

Lucy made a face at Kezzie as she followed him obediently out of the room Kezzie gave her sister a warning look After some time, when they didn't reappear, both she and Lady Fitzwilliam went to look for them They found Lucy and William sitting upstairs surrounded by an enormous variety of exotic clothes. capes and wigs, long dresses, fans and parasols, pirate costumes, cowboy outfits

Lady Fitzwilliam clapped her hands 'I'd forgotten all about these clothes,' she exclaimed 'It is so long since there've been young children in this house '

'Let's play charades,' declared William

It was a game Lucy had never played before, but she proved to have a great talent for acting She and William had the most tremendous fun and, working together, managed to win most of the time Kezzie and Lady

Fitzwilliam eventually called a halt to the game, which would have gone on all night

'Did you enjoy that?' Kezzie asked her sister as they prepared for bed.

'It was jolly good,' said Lucy

Kezzie burst out laughing

'I still don't know what he is saying half the time,' Lucy confided, 'but now I just say "yes" and nod a lot He seems to like that.'

The next day they made a picnic and went to the seaside It was many miles before they reached the flat fen country

'Don't be too excited,' William warned them as they approached King's Lynn There are huge concrete blocks and barbed wire and anti tank devices all over the beaches, but we might find a place to get on to the sands'

How beautiful England is, thought Kezzie, as they passed the little villages, the country pubs and steepled churches with weathercocks on top It seemed such a desecration when they reached the coast and saw the defences against the expected invasion The ugly rolls of jagged wire, and the danger signs with skull and crossbones painted on In some areas land mines had been planted to slow down or repel approaching enemy tanks Kezzie shuddered Thank God, it hadn't come to that Churchill was right The whole of Britain owed the RAF an unimaginable debt

They found a place among the dunes to eat their sandwiches, and although they could not bathe they spread a rug among the tussocks of grass and sunbathed for an hour or two Lucy and Lady Fitzwilliam made sandcastles Kezzie watched them together as her eyes closed drowsily Such friends they had become, crossing barriers of age and class with apparent ease William joined them in their game, constructing a moat and a drawbridge and bossing them both like a spoiled child Kezzie's eyes closed as she relaxed into sleep, head propped against some cushions.

It was dusk when they started for home. On the journey back Lucy cuddled in against Lady Fitzwilliam on the rear seat. At one stage Kezzie turned around to say something and then stopped. They were both asleep, their foreheads and cheeks pink where they had caught the sun.

William stretched across and grasped Kezzie's hand. 'It was so good of you to come all the way down here and spend some time with Ma,' he said. 'You and Lucy have been a tonic. She is much more cheerful than when I saw her last.'

Kezzie smiled at him. 'No,' she said, 'it is your mother who has helped us. When I came at first I could scarcely stand up. She looked after us both.'

'Tonight we will go to a dance,' William told Kezzie when they arrived at the house. 'There's a forces' base a few miles east of Nottingham. I know one or two chaps there. I don't know if I'll actually get you on the floor, but at least we can listen to the music.'

'I don't have anything to wear,' said Kezzie.

'Nonsense,' said Lady Fitzwilliam, who had overheard their conversation. 'We will find something suitable.'

She searched through her own wardrobe until she came across a blue silk dress patterned with tiny rosebuds.

'We will have to shorten the skirt,' she told Kezzie. 'You have a bath, my dear, and I will see how rusty my sewing skills are.' She smiled. 'This length was very daring when I wore it. I was the first young lady in the county to reveal some leg – quite scandalous at the time.'

In fact, when she reached the army base and went into the room where the band was playing Kezzie realised that she needn't have worried about her dress at all. Many women were there in uniform, or wearing a plain skirt and cardigan. The idea was to relax and forget the war for a short time She sat at a table and sipped lemonade while William went to the bar for a beer

Shortly before it ended Kezzie persuaded William onto the floor He was self-conscious about his leg, but she insisted that he should partner her for the last waltz

On the way home William spoke to Kezzie quite seriously It is such a great comfort to me to know that Ma has you with her when I am away,' he said Promise me that you'll stay on a little longer '

He parked the jeep in front of the house and helped her out Just as she stepped from the running board he lifted her into his arms and kissed her gently She waited, quite still, as he put his fingers in her hair and stroked her face Then he crushed her head tightly against his chest She knew that they understood each other quite well He was the brother she never had, and she was a sister He kept her very close to him for many minutes, as if clinging on to some vibrant contact with life, knowing that when dawn came he would have to face death once more

The next morning they got up early to wave William off on the long drive south to rejoin his fighter squadron He kissed them all again many times, and shook hands warmly with Samuel, who stood on the bottom step holding his kitbag His eyes were shining as he turned and waved once last time before switching on the engine and letting out the clutch The jeep shot off at speed and soon disappeared between the stone pillars

'You know,' said Lady Fitzwilliam to Kezzie 'I do believe he is desperately keen to get back to his base and into the air again '

They waited in front of the house until the sound of the horn and the noise of the engine faded Lady Fitzwilliam shivered slightly as they turned to go back to the house She looked at the sky

'Sun has gone in,' she said

# 25

# Bad News

The first chestnuts were falling and fields were the colour of baked biscuit when the local farmer called round at the house and reminded Kezzie of her promise.

'Working on a farm!' said Lady Fitzwilliam when Kezzie told her. She pressed her lips together. 'I thought you had intentions of becoming a doctor?'

'I have,' said Kezzie. 'And I will,' she added. 'But at the moment they need help to bring the harvest in. There are not many people who can drive the tractor and it will only be for a few weeks,' she reassured Lady Fitzwilliam.

On the first day she began work Kezzie dressed as she had seen the other land-girls do. The farmer's wife had given her some heavy-duty clothes to wear. Kezzie combed her hair and tucked all of it right up under a scarf, which she tied in a bandanna style around her head. Then she put on the rough checked shirt, the thick brown dungarees, and the dark green wellington boots. She went downstairs to the kitchen where Lucy and Lady Fitzwilliam were having breakfast together.

'Well,' said Kezzie, turning about to show off her outfit, 'what do you think?'

There was a silence. Then Lucy giggled and Lady Fitzwilliam breathed deeply, then cleared her throat. 'It's not really what one would call . . . em . . . *pretty*? Is it, my dear?' she enquired politely.

Kezzie laughed out loud. 'Dungarees aren't meant to be pretty,' she said. 'I think their designer had a more functional use in mind.'

Lady Fitzwilliam sighed. 'Oh well,' she said. 'I read the

other day that the Princess Margaret was wearing a boiler suit. So, one must adapt to the times, I suppose

Impulsively Kezzie went over and hugged her 'Wish me luck,' she said. 'I am so nervous '

'Gracious, child, what have you to be nervous about?'

Kezzie shrugged. 'I don't know,' she replied 'I might not be able to keep up with the rest of the girls I could have an accident with the tractor . . all sorts of things '

Lady Fitzwilliam stood up 'You'll manage perfectly well,' she asserted firmly. 'Just be careful that you don't develop . . . muscles.'

The work was hard and each minute of daylight precious The girls rose before dawn and were in the fields as the first light of the sun was edging over the horizon They worked together in a cheerful group of mixed personalities and backgrounds. And they knew how to enjoy themselves. There wasn't a dance or singsong or get-together within a radius of twenty miles that they didn't hear of or wangle an invitation to Despite an aching back Kezzie was enjoying herself She loved being outdoors, driving in the fields and cycling home at night Often she would stop for a few minutes before putting her bike away to watch the long-drawn-out sunsets, the western sky painted in vertical lines of blues and reds

Kezzie liked the colours of autumn, and the harmony of the land and nature that produced the harvest filtered into her spirit. The screeching, scavenging crows settling in a noisy cloud behind her as her tractor moved down the furrow, the clods tumbling behind as the blades sliced through the dun-coloured earth Many of the farms had gone back to using horse-drawn ploughs, the huge shires making their stately way up and down the field

She was sleeping well, and eating better than she had done for many months There was something satisfying about the sight of the hay stooks and the smell of the apples in the brown wooden barrels Honeysuckle grew around the barn door and blue and yellow gladioli stood on long green stalks in front of the white-painted farmhouse And the land girls with their chat and laughter became part of the landscape itself The farmer's wife was delighted with their company and her husband declared he had never had better workers

The other bonus for Kezzie was the fact that she was paid a wage It wasn't very much, but Kezzie felt that at least she could contribute something to her and Lucy's upkeep The farmer also gave her potatoes and turnips to bring home She knew that Lady Fitzwilliam would not accept any of the money she earned She had tried tentatively to bring the subject up but it had been dismissed abruptly 'My husband left me quite comfortably off. William and I are well provided for, and indeed, Samuel also So there is no need to discuss the matter further '

However, her income gave Kezzie some independence She was able to buy some small things for herself and Lucy She occasionally went to the clothing exchange in the nearest town Lady Fitzwilliam had at first been very reluctant to accompany them, but eventually her curiosity proved too strong and she came along. To her astonishment there were several other titled ladies rummaging through the assorted bundles

'I consider it my patriotic duty,' one declared loudly We are being exhorted to "make do and mend" and that's what I intend to do '

'They say it's saving our merchant fleet They are in enough danger transporting essential foods,' said another

Later, when Kezzie looked across the church hall, she saw Lady Fitzwilliam arguing with someone over possession of a hat She finally came towards Kezzie clutching it firmly in one hand.

'Surely we can fight a war without rationing hats,' she said.

Kezzie obtained some shoes, a cardigan and an old army blanket from which she intended to make Lucy a winter coat. The weather was becoming severe and Kezzie was glad that they had the foresight to lay up supplies of wood. People were scavenging for coal in old bings, and along the seashore.

Kezzie knew from the newspaper reports that Michael had been in action again. As the Germans were moving so fast through Greece his unit had been sent quickly from Egypt to the southern coast of Crete. They took up a position on the Plain of Messara to defend the island from the expected invasion. Enemy paratroopers were dropped in great numbers and the British were forced to withdraw in confusion. Some were left behind, but Michael was with the detachment who reached Heraklion and were picked up by the Royal Navy. The ships were bombed heavily, and less than half of the battalion returned to Egypt.

> *We're having a wonderful holiday*, he had written to Kezzie. *We try out all the beaches. Unfortunately some other people want the place to themselves. They're not so keen on our company, and don't like sharing. So most times one or other of us has to go. This time it was us . . .*

Kezzie kept the letter in the pocket of her shirt and took it out to read from time to time. He had been in terrible danger and she hadn't known anything about it. She knew now the bond that she and Lady Fitzwilliam shared and why, every time she raised the subject of returning to Scotland, William's mother tried to persuade her to stay a little longer.

'Wait until the New Year,' she had begged Kezzie, 'until we are certain that there will be no more air raids, and things are more settled in Clydebank.'

Kezzie knew that they had become very close, and the older woman would miss her and Lucy dreadfully when they finally went home.

Towards the end of the year women between the ages of twenty and forty were called up. Lady Fitzwilliam's maid Sally went off and joined the WRNS. Kezzie was rising early, and working late, storing the last of the crop for the winter, so that it was Lucy who had to instruct Lady Fitzwilliam in the basic skills of cooking and keeping house. Kezzie marvelled at the development in her sister. She was becoming very competent in many practical things, and did not seemed so troubled now by new and strange experiences. One day Samuel managed to shoot a rabbit. He came in and very proudly presented the carcass to Lucy and Lady Fitzwilliam in the kitchen.

'And what am I supposed to do with this?' Lady Fitzwilliam demanded, gazing with deep repugnance upon the dead animal.'

'We need a sharp knife,' said Lucy. 'A *very* sharp knife.'

Lady Fitzwilliam shuddered. She stood up quickly. 'I shall be in the conservatory, if you require me,' she said.

It was left to Lucy to skin the rabbit, and joint and cook it. That night Kezzie could smell the savoury stew as she opened the back door. She sat down wearily on the steps and pulled her boots off.

'Something smells delicious,' she said.

'I did it all by myself,' said Lucy proudly. 'Everything. Prepared the food, peeled the vegetables, cooked the stew. All of it.'

'So we're going to have a feast,' said Kezzie.

The doorbell rang as Lady Fitzwilliam was laying the table and setting out the dishes. Kezzie crossed to the small stone sink in the corner to wash up before dinner, and Samuel went to answer the front door. Kezzie was drying her hands on a towel when she noticed that Samuel was standing just inside the doorway leading through to the hall. He stood very still, as though he had been there many moments, she thought. Almost at the same moment Lady Fitzwilliam looked up and saw him.

'Samuel, you startled me,' she said. 'I didn't see you there.'

'You have a visitor, ma'am,' Samuel announced slowly. 'The Wing Commander from Master William's squadron is in the drawing room.'

Kezzie realised that the old man was carefully avoiding looking directly at either Lady Fitzwilliam or herself. He was staring stolidly at a point beyond their heads. 'The gentleman says he would like a word with you,' said Samuel. 'In private.'

Lady Fitzwilliam carefully put the plate she was holding onto the table. 'Kezzie,' she said, 'please accompany me.'

'Missing – believed killed.'

Lady Fitzwilliam repeated the words the Wing Commander had just said. He looked at her anxiously, and then at Kezzie.

'Some water?' he suggested.

Lady Fitzwilliam shook her head. 'No,' she said. 'No . . . thank you. Please tell me the details.'

'He was part of a flight arm escorting a group of RAF bombers on a sortie into France. They crossed the French coast south of Le Touquet and ran into an enemy patrol. There was a brief dogfight. He downed at least one Messerschmitt, before being struck himself. His plane exploded on impact. No one baled out. I am sorry. He was a wonderful young man.'

Lady Fitzwilliam sat in her chair, her back straight, her head erect.

'Is there no hope?' she asked. 'Can you give me no hope? None at all?'

'It is very unlikely that he has survived,' said the Wing Commander.

'But not impossible,' persisted Lady Fitzwilliam. 'Not entirely impossible?'

The Wing Commander spread his hands. 'Not entirely, no,' he agreed.

'Then I will continue to wait for my son to come home,' said Lady Fitzwilliam. Her voice shook.

Kezzie accompanied the officer to the front door. The Wing Commander spoke to her before he left. 'I have reported that he is "missing in action: believed killed".'

He looks enormously weary, thought Kezzie. She placed her hand on his arm, touching for a moment the thick gold braid of his sleeve. His eyes met hers, faded grey, with lines of exhaustion etched around the sockets.

But, like William's mother, she too needed something to cling on to.

'No,' said Kezzie. 'File it only as "missing in action". Please,' she added.

He nodded and left. Kezzie gripped the door handle tightly. 'Women weep and young men die,' she said as she closed the door behind him.

When Kezzie returned to the drawing room Lady Fitzwilliam was not weeping.

'Am I a foolish old woman?' she asked Kezzie, 'to believe that there may be the merest chance of his surviving?'

Kezzie went and knelt by her chair. 'If you are, then I am foolish too,' she said.

Kezzie's work at the farm finished and the weather hardened into bleak winter. On the 8th of December 1941 the Japanese bombed Pearl Harbour and a week later America was in the war.

# 26

# 1942: The Americans Arrive

Kezzie had collected a parcel at the railway station one morning and was tying it onto the back of her bicycle when a tall tanned soldier, with the captain's stripes of the United States Army on his sleeve, walked casually up to the ticket office. He leaned on the little wooden ledge and called through the glass partition to Mr Penrose.

'Say, buddy. D'you know anyplace hereabouts I'd get some gas?'

'Gas?' said Mr Penrose. He surveyed the young man suspiciously, taking in the strange uniform and the cropped hair, shorn all over so that the scalp gleamed through.

'Yeah, gas,' the soldier repeated.

Mr Penrose frowned at him severely. 'Are you a Germ—' he began.

'Excuse me,' said Kezzie quickly. 'I think he means petrol. Don't you?' She smiled at the American soldier. 'Gasoline for your motor car, sorry, automobile,' she said. 'We call it petrol over here.'

The officer grinned at her. 'Sounds fine by me, honey,' he said. 'Smile like that, and you can call it anything you please.'

Kezzie blushed as he stared at her boldly. She was suddenly conscious of the long dark trousers which she now wore on a regular basis. 'They're so convenient when cycling,' she had told Lady Fitzwilliam. In actual fact she found them an easier way to dress for practically every occasion. However, in order not to upset Lady Fitzwilliam too much, she did still change into a skirt for dinner.

'I can show you where there's a garage which sells petrol,' Kezzie told the American soldier.

In the background Mr Penrose tutted loudly.

Captain Joe Petrowski introduced himself as a surgeon with the American Medical Division, and offered Kezzie a ride back to the manor house. He chatted away as he lifted her bicycle into the back of his jeep and they drove along the country lanes. His accent and easy informal manner reminded her of Ricardo, and she felt suddenly, and quite sharply, homesick. She had thought of returning to Scotland at the beginning of the year. When she had discussed it with Lucy, it had been her little sister who had told her quite firmly that they should stay on for a bit.

Yes, Lucy agreed that she too missed Scotland and Aunt Bella. She would like to go back to the little café and see Peg and Ricardo, and the two signoras who had treated her so lovingly. And most especially she wanted to play with Alec, who would now no longer be a baby. 'But William's mother needs us so much, Kezzie,' said Lucy. 'She is being very brave and not complaining, but she couldn't cope on her own. She can get through the days, but she wouldn't manage the nights.'

'The nights?' said Kezzie in surprise. 'What happens at night-time?'

'Her room is next to mine,' said Lucy. 'I hear her walking up and down for hours and hours. Sometimes I go in and pretend I'm frightened and can't sleep, and then she sings to me. She reads me William's letters, and shows me old photographs, and I tell her about Granddad and his stories. You know, Kezzie, they would have been great pals,' said Lucy.

Kezzie gazed at her sister in amazement. 'You and Lady Fitzwilliam?' she said 'You help her when she is grieving for William?'

'Aunt Mary,' Lucy corrected her. 'She told me I had to stop calling her Lady Fitzwilliam. So you see, Kezzie, she needs to have someone with her.'

Kezzie marvelled at her sister, at her strength and resourcefulness, and at her perception in appreciating the similarity between the older woman and their own grandfather. Indeed, Kezzie realised, the two of them would have got on extremely well together. She could just imagine the terrific arguments and political discussions they would have had. And, Kezzie suspected, it wouldn't always have been her granddad who would have won the debate. She knew that she couldn't possibly return to Scotland just yet. It would be an act of cruelty to take Lucy away, and deprive William's mother of possibly the only person who was helping her to struggle through to each lonely dawn.

They created quite a stir when the jeep skidded to a halt below the front steps of the house. It was almost lunchtime and Lady Fitzwilliam and her helpers were ushering the children onto the trap to be driven home. One of the young mothers nudged Kezzie and whispered, 'Where did you find him? He's fabulous, absolutely gorgeous. Introduce us.'

Joe's American drawl, and his charm had an immediate effect. The young woman giggled and, gazing up at him, said 'Well, if you're around here, I, for one, am going to feel a lot safer at night.'

'That is an opinion not everyone might share,' Lady Fitzwilliam observed drily. 'In particular that young woman's husband,' she added under her breath to Kezzie.

They invited Joe to stay for lunch and as he came through the house he stared openly at everything. He was fascinated by it all. The wide corridors, the tapestries, the curved stairway and huge rooms.

'Gee, would you look at this.' He looked around the kitchen, and touched the row of bells which had been used for calling the servants. 'It's for real! I thought you only saw these kinda things in the movies.'

Lucy watched him closely throughout the meal. He at once cut all his food up into small pieces. Then he put down his knife and, transferring his fork to his right hand, he began to eat.

Kezzie saw Lady Fitzwilliam raise her eyebrows. Not all the American ways were going to be welcome in Britain, she thought.

She was proved correct. The American soldier's weekly pay equalled around seven pounds sterling, while the ordinary British private earned not much more than seven shillings. They called their uniforms Government Issue, so the British began calling the soldiers themselves GIs. All of them spoke, and a good many of them looked, like cinema stars. They brought their own supplies and were able to procure fruit, nylon stockings, and chocolate – things which hadn't been seen in Britain for years. They were hugely popular with lots of young women. Quite understandably, many British men loathed them.

Their presence struck the surrounding area like a multi-coloured firework. Lucy, to Lady Fitzwilliam's consternation, started using American slang. When she was cooking eggs she enquired if they preferred them 'overeasy' or 'sunny side up' and she would shout, 'Got any gum, chum?' when Joe appeared at the back door.

He became a frequent visitor to the house. He was establishing what he called a back-up base at an old aerodrome a few miles away. The United States Medical Corps was setting up a series of hospital units all over the country. They were located away from the major cities for fear of bomb damage, but near transport lines and railway stations. West Fenton was an ideal place to have one.

'We're going to have more and more casualties as the war goes on,' Joe told them. 'From bombing missions, from active service units in the major conflicts abroad, and when the big push comes next year or the year after. The first-aid posts in the field can only do so much, and the British hospitals at home won't be able to cope. We'll pick up on the more serious cases which will be flown back.'

He was very proud of having his operating theatre in working order so quickly. They had done one emergency appendectomy on the small son of the owner of the village inn. The appendix had been on the point of bursting and the doctor let it be known that, but for Joe and his team, the child might have died. After this incident the Americans found that the local people treated them in a more friendly manner.

Not long after, when Joe was having dinner at the house, and he was telling them about some new technical apparatus which had arrived, Kezzie recalled Dr McMath speaking of the same piece of equipment. She commented on this to Joe, and he began to ask her about her work at the pharmacy in Canada.

'We'll need more staff if things hot up,' he said, 'and I'd like someone who has had practical experience. I could train you just now as a theatre assistant.

Kezzie's hands began to shake. She put her knife and fork down carefully. 'You don't mean it, do you?' she asked him. 'Would you actually take me on?'

'Sure,' he said. 'We could give it a try.'

# 27
# US Hospital

Kezzie found that the hospital demanded all her energy. It was the most difficult work she had ever undertaken. Not only physically and mentally, but also emotionally.

When the first wounded began to arrive, isolated cases who were casualties from bombing sorties, she found the very youth of the patients distressing. The broken remnants of the young men would have caused the stoutest spirit to falter. It was a strain to be cheerful while nursing a boy, little older than herself, whose leg or arm, or both, had been amputated.

Joe was ruthlessly efficient and demanded the same standard from his staff that he gave himself.

'We're gonna be the best,' he said. 'That's the target. Nothing lower.'

He was training her in theatre skills and had bawled her out on several occasions for what he considered sloppy work. She found it hard to reconcile this Joe with the big easy-going guy who loved to clown around with Lucy and the rest of the children at the house. He was full of energy. No matter how hard the week had been at the hospital, the weekend always found him out dancing somewhere. Jitterbugging or waltzing round the floor crooning in her ear, 'Don't sit under the apple tree with anyone else but me . . .'

When she wasn't on duty he plied her with textbooks and medical journals to read. She was learning fast under his direction. Lady Fitzwilliam was enthusiastic about the whole situation.

'You can apply to take a pre-university entrance exam course in the autumn,' she told Kezzie. 'We will write off now and find out what preparation you might have to do.'

And so it seemed to Kezzie that for the time being her life had been settled for her. Lucy was happy, more content than she had ever been, in fact. Lady Fitzwilliam would be bereft if they moved away. And her own future . . . there was now a real possibility that her dream of becoming a doctor could come true.

While Kezzie worked in the hospital, Lady Fitzwilliam and Joe were making plans together.

'This house is under-utilised,' she had declared to Kezzie one day.

Kezzie knew that this was Joe's influence. He found the enormous empty rooms at odds with his own cramped quarters in what was essentially Nissen hut accommodation.

'We could have patients to convalesce here,' said Lady Fitzwilliam.

She had now almost completely handed over the daily lessons in the house to the childrens' parents. There was hope that the local school might reopen after Easter as someone knew of a former teacher who was to be invalided out of the RAF. Joe was keen to see this happen. He, more than any of them, realised how many more beds would be needed for the wounded as the war went on.

'Kezzie, Lucy, Samuel and myself can move up to the attic rooms,' Lady Fitzwilliam told him. 'We will store the furniture and then we could adapt the remaining space as an overflow from your unit.'

They had discussed ideas, the possibility of converting the dining room into a general ward and making the conservatory into a day room.

Some of Lady Fitzwilliam's county friends had been taken aback by the prospect of her actual involvement in the wounded convalescing in the house

'We thought you would have a more supervisory role, Mary,' had been the comment. 'You're not thinking of nursing the patients yourself, are you, dear? Do you realise that you may be asked to bathe or change some of these soldiers . . . *male* soldiers.'

'I think they imagined me walking about with a lamp at night and the men kissing my shadow on their pillow as I passed,' Lady Fitzwilliam said to Kezzie at dinner one evening. 'I just told them, "If you mean shit and smelly socks, then I'm perfectly capable of dealing with both. I can clean up dung as well as anyone else, don't you know".

Kezzie choked on her food. 'You didn't actually say that, did you?'

'I certainly did,' declared Lady Fitzwilliam. 'I may not be invited to tea at the vicarage again.'

And she was doing it. There was no task that she considered too menial for her to perform. She had one particular boy who was quite clearly her favourite. He had developed gangrene in both his legs. She emerged from his room one night after cleaning his wound and changing his dressing. She caught Kezzie watching her as she rinsed out the foul bandages.

'You should take some time off,' Kezzie suggested. 'You could exhaust yourself. You do so much.'

Lady Fitzwilliam smiled at her wearily. 'My only hope is that someone somewhere is taking care of William,' she said.

Kezzie took the linen out of her hands. 'Come and have some tea,' she said.

Kezzie felt quite humbled by the way this woman had coped with the many trials of her life and how well she adapted to the fantastic changes in her world and experience. From oil lamp, through gas, to electric power; from gramophone records to radio links which flashed around the world in seconds She had stepped from one century to the next, watching an empire, which she and her kind had helped create, now slowly fragmenting and disintegrating. Things would never be the same again. Lady Fitzwilliam herself recognised this fact and had the wisdom to see that some changes were necessary and might perhaps be beneficial.

She talked to Kezzie about the role of women in society.

'I knew Emmeline Pankhurst slightly,' she said. 'I'd always thought . . .' Lady Fitzwilliam hesitated, 'that she made such a dreadful fuss about issues which most women were not the least concerned with Now, I'm not so sure.'

'It will be different after this,' said Kezzie. 'There are nurseries for children and these will continue. It will give women more freedom.'

Lady Fitzwilliam sighed 'I never imagined that I would hear myself say this,' she said 'But, I do hope you're right, my dear.'

The civilian restrictions continued. In April the Government banned embroidery on women's underwear and nightwear. Joe thought this was very funny. 'How the hell are they gonna police this ordinance? I want to be the first guy to volunteer for duty as enforcement officer for that law.' He nodded and grinned at Lucy. 'I'll just have to approach ladies on the sidewalk and say, "Pardon me, ma'am, but I'm obliged to inspect your underwear. It's a government rule".'

Lady Fitzwilliam frowned severely as Lucy giggled.

The war news however was not good. Joe read the newspapers and commented to Kezzie, 'We're gonna have lots of customers very soon.'

In Russia Sebastopol had fallen, and in the Western Desert Rommel's Afrika Korps struck. The Argyll and Sutherland troops, with armour and infantry from

Australia, New Zealand, South Africa and India, were now part of Lieutenant-General Montgomery's Eighth Army in Egypt. At the end of May, in a great tank battle at Bir Hacheim, the Germans tried to turn the British southern flank. In the middle of June Tobruk fell and twenty-five thousand Allied soldiers were captured. At the end of the month the British Army had to abandon Mersa Matruh in Egypt. Six thousand more prisoners were taken by the Germans. Rommel with his twelve divisions was within seventy miles of Alexandria and the Nile.

Kezzie fell ill. There had been no word from Michael for weeks and weeks. She had received his last letter at the beginning of March and it had been written around Christmas-time.

He had told her of the beauty of the desert countries, the exotic dress of the natives, the strange languages, and the stillness and deepness of the dark blue nights. The sky and earth so close to each other. The feeling of history, of ancient and honoured traditions. He now felt that the Western powers were imposing on these people, demanding that they change to a lifestyle which they neither wanted nor needed. 'Theirs is a future of exploitation,' he wrote to her.

Kezzie realised that Michael was thinking deeply, as she had, about the ultimate purpose of the war. He, like her, was aware of the significant changes which were taking place, of how society was altering, had altered already. And despite its being a frightening prospect, it was important that this time they tried to set the world right as best they could.

The German panzer divisions rolled on. Backed up by devastating aerial bombardment they advanced more than three hundred miles. By late summer the Allied troops were left defending a narrow front along the Quattara depression. At a place called El Alamein the Eighth Army grimly held the line

The more serious casualties were being flown home, the dead and the dying The reputation of Joe's surgical unit was becoming widely known Generally they only received grievously wounded men, and as the summer progressed they became busier and busier.

At the beginning of autumn they were working and operating all round the clock. Late one night Kezzie was taking a patient out of theatre. As she stopped in the ante-room to connect the transfusion unit, another soldier was brought it. The junior doctor checked him over quickly. He shook his head and handed the clipboard with the case notes back to the stretcher-bearer.

'This one's a goner,' said the orderly to his friend, and began to turn the wheels around.

Kezzie pressed herself against the wall to make room for them to leave. As the trolley slid past her she glanced down at the wounded man The bottle of blood she was holding slipped from her fingers and crashed to the floor.

'No!' she said. 'Oh God. No.'

Kezzie was looking on the pale still face of Michael Donohoe.

# 28
# Life or Death

'What's up?' Joe Petrowksi appeared at the door of his operating theatre.

'I think this one's gone, sir,' said the junior doctor.

Kezzie uttered a low cry. From behind her clenched teeth came a supressed scream. She clutched at herself, wrapping her arms around her own body tightly. She was breaking apart, all of her, physically and mentally, her heart and her life, her very spirit, was disintegrating, and she could not control it.

'No,' she whispered. 'No.'

'Nurse, pull yourself together,' said the matron. 'We've got other patients here who would profit from your help.'

'No,' Kezzie said again.

The world was spinning . . . the whole great globe . . . never-ending, into eternity, and she herself was dying. She knew this. Before her eyes Michael's life force was ebbing away, and with it, so was hers.

If there ever had been any doubt at all that this man, who now lay so cold and still before her, was part of her own being, then it was gone. They were inextricably linked. From the very first moment, when his eyes had met hers at the autumn harvest in Stonevale, there had been no other path for her to take but the one that joined with his. No other course for either of them. She had kept the memory of it all in her heart. The gulls crying above them as they lifted the crop together from the ochre earth. The music and the tales around the fire. The smell and the sound of both their languages and cultures bonding together. Connected by fate, separated by circumstance and war, was death now to part them for ever?

'Kezzie!'

Her glazed eyes hardly registered what was happening. The name being called did not connect to her.

'Kezzie!' Captain Joe Petrowski cried again. 'Is this guy a friend of yours?'

She inclined her head.

Joe nodded at his staff. 'Bring him in.'

The stretcher attendants exchanged glances 'Sir, it's not going to be worth the trouble.'

'Her face says it is,' the captain said curtly.

The junior doctor hesitated. 'Sir . . .'

'Wheel him in,' Joe snapped. Then he leaned over and spoke to Kezzie. 'I need an experienced assistant in there,' he said. 'So c'mon, clean up and help me.'

She stared at him.

'You hear me?' he shouted into her face. 'Pick up or get out!'

He turned and strode through the open doors.

She followed him more slowly.

'Get me plasma,' he ordered.

'I can't,' she whispered.

He changed his gloves in seconds. Then he looked at her before he pulled his mask on. 'I'm not carrying passengers,' he said. 'Don't come in here if you can't handle it. There are no free rides on this trip.'

Inside the theatre they were cutting off Michael's uniform.

'Gee, what a mess,' said the junior doctor. 'What a bloody mess. It's all in his chest. One lung gone, definitely.' He looked questioningly at the surgeon.

Joe Petrowski nodded. If he was worried he didn't show it. 'I guess we're gonna have to work to hold him then,' he said. 'Let's do it.'

It was the hardest thing Kezzie had ever done Fingers slippery with sweat, every part of her cringing as she saw the torn flesh. She could barely watch as the rubber bag began to rise gently as they tried to reinflate Michael's lung and get him breathing again. She knew she had to function, and fast, or Joe would throw her out.

'I'm needed,' she told herself. She held her hands rigid to prevent them shaking. 'Joe needs me.'

And Michael needed her too She was the most experienced assistant on duty. She had to stay, do what she was trained to do. Be detached, professional. She had wanted to be a doctor for as long as she could remember. Now was the time to prove she was capable. She had to do it.

And suddenly she was keeping up with Joe's instructions, watching his hands, listening to his voice. She took her lead from him The way he moved and how he handled the equipment. His actions not slow, but deliberate and sure. Cool, competent and efficient, even at the most difficult parts. He removed the shrapnel and cut out the dead and damaged tissue.

Only at one point, when Michael's heart stopped again, did he say in exasperation, 'Aw c'mon, buddy. You're gonna have to do a bit of this yourself.'

He grinned at Kezzie as the faltering pulse came back. It was the first time he had looked directly at her since he had begun to operate.

'What's his name?' he asked her.

'Michael.'

'OK, Michael,' he said. 'I'd sure appreciate for you not to do that again.' He glanced around. 'We'll close now,' he told his team. He looked at Kezzie again. 'Then it all depends on how much fighting spirit this guy's got.'

'How much fighting spirit, have you got, Michael?' Kezzie whispered as she watched him being transferred to the recovery room. She followed the trolley down the corridor, and stood by his bed. How much? she wondered.

She wouldn't leave him. Not at all during the long days and longer nights which followed. She talked to him as she changed his drip. His hand was so cold when she reinserted the needle under the vein in his arm.

'Michael,' she said softly.

Lady Fitzwilliam understood Kezzie's terror. She knew Kezzie's fear was that Death stalked the corridors at night, and if she was not watchful then it would come for Michael. If she allowed herself to slip into sleep for one moment then it would steal him away, and when she awoke he would be gone.

So Lady Fitzwilliam didn't tell her to come home and rest, or advise her to leave his side. She brought an easy chair into Michael's room and tucked a great blanket around Kezzie. She made tea and sat and drank it with her or stayed out in the corridor within call, all through the dark watches of those first few nights. Joe checked him every hour. Kezzie knew that he had left word to be called at any moment, day or night, if Michael's condition changed.

And all the friends she had made since arriving in England contacted the hospital. The parents of the local children, the farm workers, and Lady Fitzwilliam's colleagues on her various committees sent words of comfort. Flowers and gifts, and offers of help came from all over the country. Kezzie was overwhelmed by their kindness.

'His colour is so poor,' she complained to Lady Fitzwilliam on the third day. 'His face has such a lifeless pallor.'

'We must not expect too much,' said Lady Fitzwilliam, 'and it would be so terribly cruel to give you hope when there might be none. But . . . that skin tone does not always mean the worst. A rosy glow on someone's face can be much more deceptive and sinister.' She sighed deeply. 'I lost three babies before I had William Not one of them survived more than a year That was their colour before they died It was almost as though they were preparing to go. I often thought that it was some small kindness of the Almighty as they were about to be taken.'

As Kezzie looked at Michael, lying there so cold and still, she had an urge to pull all the tubes and tags aside and climb into bed with him. To lie down beside him and warm his body with her own.

Harvest-time was drawing to a close. The winter nights were closing in and the weather was much colder. About a week after his operation Kezzie noticed a very slight alteration in Michael's condition. During the day his body seemed less inert as she tended him, as if he were on a slightly higher level of consciousness Kezzie was worried. Joe was operating and would be unavailable for at least another hour. She gazed at Michael and called his name softly, but there was no response. His breathing was different, not so shallow, but not as regular either. Did that indicate an improvement? Was he getting better? Or was she in fact deceiving herself? She remembered what Lady Fitzwilliam had told her. This change in Michael could be the last kind act of the Creator, easing him into the afterlife.

At five o'clock she switched on the small lamp by his bed and went to close the curtains. The sun was setting over the frosted fields. A red-gold ball of fire turning the whole sky crimson, the rays shafting into the room, reflecting on the walls and ceiling. Kezzie pulled down the blind and as she turned from the window she heard a voice speaking.

'Sure, I should have known that when I died and went to heaven, the first angel's face I'd see would look like Kezzie Munro.'

# 29
# Recovery

Kezzie's heart turned over. 'Oh, Michael,' she said softly. She walked slowly from the window towards the bed and looked down at him. She smiled. 'Michael,' she said again.

His face was palest white with long shadows under his eyes, and his features were quite gaunt; the outline of cheekbones, nose and neck emphasising the hollows elsewhere. But his eyes were watching her carefully. And it was those eyes, dark, dark blue with a slightly troubled expression, more than his voice, or his colour, or the change in his breathing, that gave Kezzie hope. He gazed at her, and she could see comprehension and life slowly returning in his look.

'I'm alive,' he said at last.

'Yes.' She could barely speak the word, her chin and face were trembling so much.

He tried to raise his hand on the coverlet of the bed but could not. He tried to lift his head a little but failed completely. He sank back down. 'And I'm not imagining you?' he asked.

She sat down on the edge of the bed and took one of his hands in both of her own. 'I'm real enough, Michael Donohoe,' said Kezzie.

'I dreamt I was dead,' he said at last.

'You almost were,' she said.

'Am I all of a piece?' he asked her.

'There's a bit of you inside which will never be the same, but the doctor says you'll be able to sing and dance as well as ever you did.'

This time he managed a faint grin. 'Sure now, my prize-winning days are not over yet then,' he murmured.

He drifted into sleep.

Kezzie went to the door, opened it and slipped quietly out to the corridor. She walked sedately in the direction of the matron's office, but had gone no more than two hundred yards down the corridor before she began to run.

Joe ordered her to take some days off, but she couldn't stay away from the hospital. She sat beside Michael and held his hand, whether he was conscious or not. And slowly, slowly, his condition improved.

She told him of Canada and Clydebank. Of her return to Scotland and her friends in the café. She described the destruction of the blitz, and he wept with her when she spoke of her grandfather.

He spoke of being in combat, the vibration in the air and on the earth when they were under bombardment. The great gulping fear, inside your head and the taste in your mouth. And more than that, the terror that you might let your comrades down, that when the moment came you would not manage to fight. And the ultimate horror of seeing his friends fall beside him. She tried to comfort him, to reason away the distress he felt because now he was safe at home. He knew that Montgomery was preparing his own offensive and he wouldn't be there, his Battalion would march forward without him.

At times the war in Africa and the Far East seemed far away and remote as Kezzie cycled home across this soft landscape, with the pretty farmhouses tucked in the folds of the hills. Then they would have a rush of wounded to the hospital, and the hard reality would surface again. Kezzie was very aware of Lady Fitzwilliam's own position. With William gone it could have been awkward for her to rejoice in Michael's recovery, and very easy to resent someone else's happiness. But she didn't. She and Lucy were a solid unit behind Kezzie, helping and supporting her when she needed them the most. And as Kezzie watched the two of them together she realised that she had lost part of her sister to this woman. Lucy was the daughter Lady Fitzwilliam had never had.

They had news from Scotland. Peg and Ricardo were going to be married. They planned to have the wedding after Christmas and she and Lucy would be attendants. Peg was having trouble in obtaining any pretty clothes, and had been looking through the shops in Glasgow for lace and veil. Lady Fitzwilliam and Lucy searched the attics for anything that might do.

'Peg is tall, almost an inch more than me,' said Kezzie, 'with lovely long slim legs, and a neat waist. Her hair is the colour of fresh honey.'

'My hair was blonde once upon a time,' said Lady Fitzwilliam. 'When the regiment was in India people there used to ask my husband's permission to touch it.'

She looked out a beautiful sari folded away in tissue paper, a piece of Kashmiri cloth, and some chiffon scarves. In a decorated tin box they discovered a pair of cream buckram boots decorated with a bow which had tiny seed pearls sewn on. Joe turned up with a piece of parachute silk, but refused to divulge its source. Lady Fitzwilliam made all of their finds up into a parcel and sent Samuel off to the station to despatch them to Scotland. In her reply to thank them Peg said that she and Ricardo intended to emigrate to the United States as soon as they could.

*'It's not that I don't love Scotland,'* Peg wrote. *'It's just that Ricardo has told me so many wonderful things about America, and I have so many painful memories here.'*

Kezzie knew how she felt. She too had a great longing to go back to Canada. She was sure she would do so one day.

Joe came in a few days later to give Michael a thorough checkover.

'I'm sending you up to the big house tomorrow,' he said. 'Lady F. can take care of you We need this bed for guys who are really sick.'

'So I'm a lot better?' said Michael He was sitting propped up in bed. 'How bad is this, only having one lung?' he asked.

'Well,' said Joe pulling his stethoscope from his ears, 'you ain't gonna jitterbug no more.'

'I didn't – what was it you said? – "jitterbug" in the first place,' said Michael.

'Then you're not going to miss it much, are you?' said Joe.

Michael glanced at Kezzie 'Anything else . . . that I might miss?' he asked casually, keeping his eyes on Joe all the time.

'Well,' said Joe. 'You can't smoke You can't drink He thought for a moment. 'You can go with women.' He grinned and looked at Kezzie 'Have babies, if you want to.'

Kezzie blushed to the roots of her hair.

Michael leaned back on his pillows. 'That's OK then,' he said.

He too was looking at Kezzie.

# 30
# New Beginning

Kezzie noticed a big improvement in Michael's health within a few days of his move to the manor house. Lady Fitzwilliam and Lucy completely spoiled him with their constant attention. There were fresh flowers in his room each day, his newspaper arrived first in the morning, and he had every little treat that was obtainable, on or off the ration.

'Bread with butter!' Kezzie exclaimed one evening, when she called in to see him on her way out to start a late shift at the hospital. She snatched the sandwich from his plate and ate a piece of it.

Michael reached over and grabbed her hand. He pulled her towards him and she was surprised at the strength in his arms.

'We're getting you up out of that bed tomorrow,' she declared as she struggled free. 'I think you are malingering.'

He watched her as she peered in his shaving mirror and tidied her hair. 'I love you,' he said.

She turned and looked into his eyes. 'I know,' she replied.

In the hospital the casualties kept coming. Meanwhile, in the Soviet Union the Russians were defending Stalingrad street by street, and house by house. In a dreadful war of attrition, they managed to regain at night what the Germans, with their superior fire-power, captured during the day. Driven right to the banks of the River Don the Soviet forces hung on desperately, fighting hand to hand.

'If they can even delay Hitler a few more weeks,' said Lady Fitzwilliam, 'then he may find, as Napoleon did, that the Russian "General Winter" is an opponent that cannot be beaten.'

In the Western Desert the Eighth Army trained its newly arrived replacement troops in desert warfare. Exercises in breaching minefields and digging in; advancing under cover of their own artillery fire, and then rushing enemy positions, were practised intensively.

One morning when Michael had managed to get downstairs and they were sitting reading quietly and listening to the radio, it was time for the news bulletin. Lady Fitzwilliam rose to turn the sound up. She glanced out of the front window as she passed by.

'Dear God,' she said.

Kezzie hurried to her side and looked out. There was a helmeted policeman cycling slowly up the driveway.

Lady Fitzwilliam bowed her head and gripped the curtain. Kezzie thought she was going to fall down. They heard the bell at the front door jangling and Samuel crossing the hall slowly to answer it.

'Please, Kezzie,' whispered Lady Fitzwilliam, 'Will you go and take the telegram? I cannot deal with it at present.'

Kezzie went out of the room. Samuel was standing by the open door, turning the flat yellow envelope over and over in his hand. He looked up as Kezzie approached him.

'This will kill her,' he said. And as he spoke, Kezzie saw that the old man was crying.

Kezzie closed the door slowly and tore open the envelope. She unfolded the thick paper and read the typewritten message . . .

And read it again.

She grabbed Samuel's arm and dragging him with her she ran back to the sitting room. Lady Fitzwilliam was still holding on to the curtain, staring out beyond the lawn and the trees, her eyes wide and unseeing.

Kezzie held up the telegram. She could hardly read the words.

'It is a message from the International Red Cross,' she said. 'William is safe in the German military hospital at St Omer in France. Injured but well. Do you hear me?' she cried out. 'William is alive! He is alive!'

She burst into tears and Samuel ran forward as Lady Fitzwilliam slumped to the floor.

It was Lucy who organised them, making tea and spreading slices of bread with a thin smear of jam. Lady Fitzwilliam unlocked a small cupboard at the side of the fireplace. She brought out a bottle of brandy.

'I was keeping this to celebrate the end of the war when it came,' she said. 'Michael, I would like you to open it just now.'

After everyone had retired for the night she sat down at her desk and taking a pen she began to write.

*'My dearest, dearest son . . .'*

That night, for the first time in many months, she slept through till the dawn.

'There is hope,' she told Kezzie the next day. 'You were right, my dear. One should never give up.'

Joe seemed to think so too. 'Hitler can't win now,' he said. 'It may take a coupla years, but he's beat. And this time we're really gonna fix it so that it doesn't happen again.'

And it appeared to Kezzie that there was hope in many other aspects of life for ordinary people. The Butler proposals and Beveridge Report, dealing with reforms in education and health care were going to lead the way to a complete change in society. A Welfare State was to be created which would abolish want, with insurance against old age and unemployment. There would be family allowances and free medical treatment for all.

The war news was also full of promise for the spring. In Russia two relief columns reached the River Don and pushed the invaders back onto the steppes. Within days it became a rout. Two weeks later, in order to save his men from starvation and in direct disobedience of Hitler's orders, the German Commander surrendered to the Red Army.

And at El Alamein Montgomery made his move. Under a blanket of heavy artillery fire the Eighth Army advanced and broke through Rommel's front line. The Germans retreated as the Allies recaptured Tobruk and pursued the Afrika Korps over a thousand miles of desert. Tripoli was taken and there was a 'Victory Parade', the very first of the war for British troops.

Michael and Kezzie were walking in the walled garden at the side of the house. He was very slow, and she became quite concerned at his leaning on her so heavily.

'You're tired,' she said.

'No.' He grinned at her. 'I like walking with my arm around you. And you have to take pity on a poor wounded soldier. Don't you now?'

She reached up and tugged his hair, then led him to a wooden bench where they sat down together.

'I'll report you to Joe, if you misbehave,' she said.

'Joe,' he repeated. He looked at her directly. 'He's very fond of you. Do you like him a lot?'

'Yes,' said Kezzie. 'And I like William too, and Ricardo, and lots of other people.'

'We haven't seen each other for such a long time,' said Michael. 'I often wondered if you'd forgotten me.' He waited a moment. 'Or perhaps, there would be someone else who was special.'

Kezzie turned and faced him. 'There was no one else,' she said. 'From the very beginning there was no one else. I loved you at that first moment, when I set eyes on you, at harvest-time in Stonevale. And I've never stopped.'

They held on to each other for a long moment.

'Can we work out some kind of future?' he asked her.

'I've had a letter from a teaching hospital, offering me a place,' said Kezzie, 'and a chance to take the university entrance exams for medicine next year.'

'I can get some kind of desk job,' said Michael. 'It's not great, but I could support you while you study.'

'You wouldn't mind that?' she asked.

'Why should I?' he said. 'I'd have my own private doctor to take care of me.' He gave her a sidelong glance. 'Your pay might not be so good, but there would be other compensations.'

Kezzie helped him to his feet and they began to walk towards the house. Churchill's latest speech seemed appropriate somehow. The two of them now would go together towards their 'new beginning'. The recent victory had been declared a day of national rejoicing. Now that there was no fear of invasion it meant that church bells could be rung to celebrate the news, to announce the surge towards the end of the war and peace.

She and Michael began to walk towards the house when she drew him to a halt.

'Listen,' said Kezzie. 'Listen.'

A sound echoed on the clear still air. It was the peal of bells. And they were ringing out from every church and steeple in the land.